D1240180

BEACHSIDE PROMISES

MARIGOLD ISLAND BOOK THREE

FIONA BAKER

Copyright © 2021 by Fiona Baker

All rights reserved. This book or any portion thereof
may not be reproduced or used in any manner whatsoever
without the express written permission of the publisher except for
the use of brief quotations in a book review.

Published in the United States of America

First Edition, 2021

fionabakerauthor.com

CHAPTER ONE

The moment Brooke Collins laid eyes on the small building in downtown Marigold with its "For Rent" sign in the window, images of her potential bakery popped into her head.

She could envision the white window frames painted pink—no, *coral*. Her sign would match, though she still wasn't sure what we wanted to name the bakery. "Brooke's Bakery" was straightforward, but expected, as was simply "Brooke's." She had a working list in her bakery notes, which were filling more and more notebook pages every day.

She let her eyes flutter closed for a moment as she tried to conjure up the energy she dreamed the bakery would have. One of her favorite memories from childhood was of going into a bakery on a school trip and getting wrapped up in the scent of fresh baked goods the moment she'd walked inside. It had smelled sweet but not cloying, although back then, she had thought that the more sugary a treat was, the better.

Her teacher, Mrs. Marsh, had ushered them into a line, and when she'd gotten to the counter, she remembered ordering an oatmeal raisin cookie. Her classmates had told her it was a cookie for old people, but Brooke hadn't cared. It had been massive, the size of her head, and had tasted heavenly. Oatmeal raisin cookies were still one of her favorite varieties, even though raisins in anything could be polarizing.

The warmth and coziness of that bakery still stuck with her as if she had walked through its doors yesterday. The day they had taken the trip had been chilly, like today, and stepping inside had been a welcome respite. Everyone in the small pastry shop had looked so happy to be there, as though they were relaxing in a second home.

Brooke wanted her bakery to have all of that and more.

She had gotten a taste of the joy that watching people eat her baked goods could bring her, and the joy it brought them in return. She imagined sending people on their way with blondies or scones, smiles on their faces, and—

"Oops, sorry!" a man said, snapping Brooke out of her daydream when he bumped into her by mistake.

"Oh! It's fine!" Brooke shook her head with a laugh, putting her hand to her chest. "That's my fault. I was totally zoning out. I shouldn't have been standing right in the middle of the sidewalk."

The man just smiled and chuckled too before walking on. Brooke started on her way again, tucking her hands into the pockets of her light jacket and glancing back at the "For Rent" sign in the window. The building was in an incredible location for a bakery—it was on a busy stretch of the downtown area, which got a lot of foot traffic, and it wasn't far from the Sweet Creamery, Marigold's favorite ice cream shop.

Even though she had been pursuing the idea of opening her own bakery more seriously lately, it still felt like a huge, unattainable vision. But most dreams were. She knew she just needed to keep chipping away at it until it became a reality.

Her phone buzzed in her purse, and she fished it out, glancing down to see Hunter Reed's name on the caller ID. A grin spread across her face before she could stop herself. His call was the perfect addition to her lovely day.

Brooke still couldn't believe that he had asked her to watch his house while he was in LA shooting his latest movie, a period piece called *Far and Away*. A few months ago, she had only seen him on television or in movies, and now they were getting to be good friends. She'd been surprised to learn that a well-known actor had moved to the small island town of Marigold, and she hadn't been all that certain she would even like him when they first met.

"Hi, Hunter!" She smiled as she pressed the phone to her ear.

"Hey! I was just calling to check in on you." Hunter's deep voice came through the line. It was surprisingly quiet on his end, so Brooke assumed he was in his trailer. "How are things in Marigold? And how's the house?"

"Everything's great! There's nothing too crazy to report. I'm just taking a walk to stretch my legs and grab a few groceries. And I might get a little ice cream to go with some blondies I made if I have time. I'm going to have them after dinner."

"Ah, those blondies." Hunter let out a longing sigh. "All I've had today is a smoothie and a sad kale salad with salmon."

"That sounds incredibly LA." She snorted, still grinning.

"It is." Brooke could hear the wry amusement in his voice. "I know your blondies are incredible, and the ice cream from the Sweet Creamery is unbelievably good, but it sounds like you're even more excited than usual. Is it just because you've got a treat to look forward to later? Or is something else up?"

"I just passed by this little commercial space for rent downtown. I think it would be the perfect place for the bakery," Brooke said. "I was staring at it and daydreaming so deeply that some guy bumped into me by accident."

Hunter laughed. "It must be great, then. What's the place look like?"

"It's adorable, even without all the little changes I'd want to make. It's right near the Sweet Creamery, actually, so I bet it would get a ton of foot traffic. The windows in the front are huge, so I could have some displays set up for people passing by to see. It's got enough space for big, comfy chairs too." She sat down on a bench outside the grocery store, tucking a strand of light blonde hair behind her ear. "I would want to add my own little twist to the paint job, but aside from that, it has everything I need. Even a commercial kitchen."

"Wow, that sounds perfect," Hunter said, and she could almost imagine his gray eyes gleaming with excitement. "If your bakery is within walking distance of the Sweet Creamery, Marigold is going to need a new dentist soon."

Brooke giggled. "Well, I don't want people to get cavities, but I'd love it if the bakery got even half the customers that the Sweet Creamery does."

"It definitely would." Hunter sounded incredibly sure, which settled Brooke's nerves. "I'm sure I could clear you out of pastries all on my own, easily."

"Ha! You always say that." Brooke felt her cheeks heat up even as she smiled. Hunter was never shy about expounding on his love for everything Brooke baked, ever since he'd bitten into one of her scones for the first time.

"Well, it's true. I've been missing my morning scones."

"Speaking of scones, I made some pumpkin ones for October that have gone over really well with the guests at the Beachside Inn. I bet you'd love them too. It's finally cooling down here, so I had to break out the pumpkin." Brooke glanced up at the trees, which hadn't fully turned yet. There were still some green leaves mixed in with the gold and red ones. "It's so pretty this time of year, but I'm dreading winter. I could use a little California weather right now."

"I'd take a pumpkin scone and a cup of coffee on a chilly day over this random spike in heat we're experiencing at the moment. It's usually much cooler by now. Well, cooler by California standards," Hunter said with a sigh. "And it doesn't help that my costumes are extremely warm."

"I bet. Nineteenth century English clothing isn't exactly breathable."

Hunter was starring in a period drama, and Brooke was already excited to see it. She had helped him get ready for the audition—as much as she *could* help with her complete lack of acting chops—and was excited that he had landed the role.

"How's filming going?" she asked.

"It's going well, sweltering costumes aside. The director seems really pleased with our work, and the entire team is great. I'm working with some amazing actors, and the crew is fantastic. We've been running on schedule nearly every single day, which is rare in this business. On some movies I've worked on, we ended up staying late all the time, and I always hated it. Besides, I became a bit of a grandpa after moving to Marigold. I got used to the quiet life, and I think I was usually in bed by nine o'clock."

Brooke chuckled, imagining Hunter in an old flannel robe and slippers, sliding into bed by nine with an old book. She couldn't quite imagine it, although the more she got to know him through their phone calls and house-sitting for him, the more *normal* she realized he was, even though he was a famous actor.

He liked his nights in and his terrible TV shows as much as everyone else. Sometimes they talked about their mutual favorites if he called in the evening. His home on Marigold was definitely expensive, but it wasn't gaudy in the slightest. He had simple things that were well made, which Brooke appreciated. Most of the brands of toiletries he'd left behind were pretty normal too, things that she knew she'd find in her brother Travis's bathroom as well.

She started to ask him about how things were going for him outside of filming when she heard another voice in the background. This one was softer and higher pitched, clearly belonging to a woman.

"Oops. Hold on a sec," Hunter murmured to Brooke.

She waited, listening to the muffled sound of the

woman's warm, melodic voice. Even though she couldn't make out the words the woman was saying, Brooke knew it must be one of his co-stars. Something in her belly tightened in a surprising way. Like jealousy, almost.

Brooke blinked and started digging around in her purse to busy her hands, shaking the feeling off. She and Hunter were just friends. He was easy to talk to, and she looked forward to hearing from him whenever he called—which happened fairly often throughout the week. But their relationship wasn't *more* than that. Hunter could talk to whoever he wanted to, and based on their past conversations about his co-stars, this actress was probably a great person.

The woman laughed and said something else, which made Hunter chuckle. Something about the way the woman laughed sounded almost flirtatious, even though Brooke had no idea what they were talking about specifically.

She popped a mint into her mouth, trying to ignore that thought too. Hunter was a nice, charming, and very attractive man. Women were probably interested in him all the time.

"Hey, sorry." Hunter's voice came in clearly again as he spoke to Brooke. "I've got to get going.

Duty calls. Talk to you later, okay? Let me know if anything happens at the house."

"Okay, sure! Have a good rest of the day shooting."

"Thanks, Brooke. Bye."

He hung up, and Brooke checked the time on her phone before she put it back into her purse. She had to get going back to the inn.

Even though she wasn't on the same street as the place with the "For Rent" sign anymore, she looked back in that direction, smiling again. Hearing Hunter's enthusiasm had only made her even more excited about everything her bakery could be.

CHAPTER TWO

Hunter tucked his phone into his pocket after he ended his call with Brooke. He was still in costume, so he made a mental note to put his phone away before they started shooting again. They couldn't get into full character, putting themselves in a nineteenth century English estate, with his phone blinking or beeping in his pocket.

"Are you sure you don't mind running lines with me quickly?" Saffron, his co-star, asked. "We have a little while until we shoot the next scene, and I want to make sure I have everything down pat."

"Of course. I'm happy to." He stood and followed her out of his trailer and back onto the soundstage.

Saffron had asked to run lines with him more

than once, and he never saw her ask anyone else. Hunter was playing a man named William Bailey, and Saffron's character, Margaret, was the widow of William's brother. Their characters interacted a good amount throughout the movie, but Hunter had a lot more scenes with the actress playing his mother.

Hunter resisted the urge to mess with his neatly styled hair when Saffron shot him a smile over her shoulder. He was quickly getting the sense that she wasn't just asking him to run lines because she wanted to nail her scenes, but more because she wanted an excuse to spend time with him. It didn't take a great detective to figure that out—she wasn't being all that subtle about her interest.

She was beautiful, just as many of his female co-stars usually were, so no matter what they did, there would probably be speculation online and in tabloids that they were dating. He had gotten used to that in his years as an actor. According to the internet, he had dated or had a fling with literally every single female co-star he'd ever had.

Mimi, his agent, would have loved to pitch the story of two actors falling for each other on set—that kind of publicity always sparked more interest in a film, even if it wasn't fully true—but Hunter just didn't feel anything beyond platonic feelings for

Saffron. That deeper romantic spark was hard for him to find.

Saffron found a quiet area in the corner of the soundstage and settled into a spot to sit, positioned as she would be when they filmed the scene. Her hair and makeup were done, but the costume department had allowed her to change back into a button-down blouse and fashionably loose jeans in their brief break, since her costume was even more restrictive than his was.

Studying her again, Hunter wondered why he didn't feel much beyond friendship toward her. Maybe in the past, when he was young and caught up in the glamour of being a Hollywood star, he would have found her attractive. She had graced the covers of numerous magazines and had a smile that lit up her famous deep blue eyes.

But now that he was older, she wasn't his type. She was a wonderful actress, one of the most talented co-stars he'd had in a long time, and she seemed like a nice person. Still, something was missing. He couldn't quite put his finger on it specifically. He gave it a little more thought and realized that she didn't feel quite as real and down to earth as a woman like Brooke did.

Brooke.

Hunter took a sip from the water bottle he'd snagged on their way over, taking a moment to gather himself before launching into the scene.

He didn't have to call Brooke as often as he did, and he knew it. His house was newly renovated, and the inspectors hadn't found anything that was likely to become a problem down the road. Plus, it was just Brooke and her kitten, Scratch, staying at his place. She was responsible and wasn't going to throw a wild party or anything like that while he was gone. She even sent him pictures of his plants to let him know how they were faring.

But he liked knowing how things were back in Marigold, which he actually felt deeply homesick for already. Things were completely different there than in LA, and he missed the slow pace. Just the commute from the condo the studio was putting him up in to the soundstage where they filmed most of the movie was more stressful than anything he'd encounter in Marigold over the course of a month.

But all the things Brooke updated him on didn't interest him nearly as much as hearing her voice did. He could always hear the energetic smile in her tone, and her zest for life was contagious.

"Ready?" Saffron asked.

Hunter centered himself, pushing his thoughts about Brooke to the side for now. "Yup, all set."

Saffron had the first line, and as soon as she spoke, Hunter felt himself slip back into character, getting swept away into the nineteenth century.

* * *

"I love these decorative pumpkins. I'm glad I got some before the farmer's market booth ran out," Angela Collins said, holding a painted white pumpkin in her hands. She looked along the built-in shelves in one of Beachside Inn's common rooms. "Where should this go?"

"How about here? We could move this boat into storage. I love it, but it definitely seems more summery, so it's a good one to swap out with the change in seasons." Her close friend and co-owner of the inn, Lydia Walker, pulled a small wooden sculpture of a boat off the shelf.

"That's perfect." Angela went on her tiptoes and put the pumpkin in the now empty space.

Angela and Lydia had been decorating the inn for fall all morning. With the leaves changing around them, they knew it was time. They had decorative gourds everywhere and had changed up their flower arrangements to reflect the season. The common room they were currently decorating had already had some fall colors in it, so Angela had spruced it up with some throw pillows embroidered with leaves. Combined with the warm spiced scent of Brooke's pumpkin scones, the room was going to be too cozy to resist.

"Looks great." Lydia stepped back, depositing the boat in a box destined for storage. "I'm glad the guests seem to appreciate these little changes based on the seasons. We just got a new review that raved about the seasonal fruit muffins."

"We did? That's fantastic!" Angela smiled, picking up another pumpkin.

Ever since Meredith Walters, a famous travel blogger, had given the Beachside Inn a five-star review, their bookings had gone up significantly. And with the new influx of guests, they'd gotten a series of new reviews, all of which had been positive so far.

"Yeah, it's one of a few new ones. I have some alerts set up for when we get reviews on travel sites and other popular travel blogs. We're getting so many, and most of them are really positive." Lydia sighed in relief. "So Water Pressure Lady's review has gotten completely buried, thank goodness."

Angela held in a horrified shudder at the

memory of the guest they would forever call Water Pressure Lady after her somewhat ridiculous claim that the water pressure in her room was horrible—despite the fact that it was working fine. Nothing had made the woman happy, even after they'd bent over backward to make sure the inn had specialty items that they'd never had before.

The silver lining was that the other customers had actually liked some of the changes Water Pressure Lady had insisted on. Her demanding nature had forced Lydia and Angela to go above and beyond, and it had ultimately had a positive impact on the inn.

"Well, that's great. I'm so glad she was just a one-off grump." Angela turned a pumpkin around to show its nicer side. "I'm glad things are going well. It's such a relief, especially after all the stress and worry of getting the inn open."

"Same here. I know we adjusted our budget to reflect a slow-down in the fall and winter, but based on our bookings, it doesn't seem like we'll slow down as much as we were expecting." Lydia shrugged and went to unfold a rich orange table runner. "I guess people still want to get away from it all, even in the fall and winter."

"Yeah. I overheard some guests saying they came

for the leaves." Angela smiled. "And I know people will want to come for the holidays. Marigold is magical at Christmas time."

She could easily imagine redecorating this room for winter too, with some lights around the windows and some decor from one of the many artisans on the island. Back in the spring, she hadn't been able to concretely imagine the inn more than two months into the future, but now she could picture the little inn in all seasons. Renovating the old building had definitely had its ups and downs, but it finally felt like they were chugging along steadily.

"Mommy!" Jake, Angela's six-year-old son, came skipping into the common room. "Can I help?"

"Of course, honey. Can you hand Lydia those orange cloths so she can put them on the tables?" Angela asked.

Jake nodded and gathered up the cloths, making a beeline toward Lydia.

"Have you decided what you want to be for Halloween yet?" Lydia asked.

Like it was for many kids, Halloween was one of Jake's absolute favorite holidays. He had been talking about his class's upcoming Halloween party for weeks and had been debating between at least five different costume ideas for the past few days with

Angela, Lydia, Brooke, or their front desk employee, Kathy. On Monday, he had been undecided between a horse and a boat. And last Angela had heard, he was leaning toward one of the many superheroes from the multitude of movies that were out.

"Yeah!" Jake handed Lydia a cloth, which she spread out on a small table. "I wanna be a race car driver! With the car too! And the helmet, like real life."

"A race car driver, huh?" Angela grimaced, a bit of the wind falling out of her sails.

If he had just gone with the driver's suit, she knew she could dig up something online or at a pop-up Halloween store. But the car and the helmet? She had no idea how to manage all of that. Based on past Halloweens she'd experienced with Jake, kids went all out these days. Angela shot Lydia a look over Jake's head, and her friend shrugged in return.

"Are you sure, buddy? What about being a ghost? Or a wizard?" Angela asked, half-joking but half-hoping he'd change his mind in favor of something she could throw together at home.

"Nope. A race car driver." Jake beamed. "No one else in my class is dressing up like one."

"Okay, then. A race car driver it is." Angela smiled, watching Jake jump around in excitement even as she wracked her brain for ways to make his dream happen in a short amount of time.

She wasn't afraid to admit that she wasn't handy in the slightest. She wasn't a great seamstress either. At most, she could put together some of Jake's most basic Lego toys and furniture, the latter of which she was at least familiar with because of her previous career as an interior decorator. But building cars was totally out of her wheelhouse.

They finished decorating the common rooms, and Jake got picked up for a play date he had with a friend who lived nearby. With their assistant Kathy manning the front desk, Angela headed into the back office and called her new boyfriend, Patrick.

They had only officially been together for about a month, but it had been one of the best months she'd had in a long time. Neither of them had expected to fall for someone new so soon after their first marriages had ended, but the longer they'd held back their feelings, the harder it had become to pretend they were just friends. Still, they were taking it slow.

"Hey, you," Patrick said when he answered the phone.

The warmth in his voice made Angela feel like she'd just taken a sip of hot cocoa on a chilly night. She grinned in spite of herself, glad that no one else was in the office to see the sappy smile spread across her face. "Hi, yourself."

"What's up?"

"Not much." She twisted a lock of her honey-blonde hair around her finger as she spoke, examining the ends. "We're just preparing for Halloween over here. Jake finally decided what he wants to be."

"Ah. He finally picked, huh? It sounded like he had a lot of potential options."

"Yeah, don't I know it. He's been changing his mind so many times that I can hardly keep up. I thought I had a decent idea of what he'd go with, but he came up with something I didn't even know he'd been considering."

"What did he go with?"

"He wants to be a race car driver—but not just any race car driver. He wants to have the suit and the helmet *and* the car, and I have no idea how we're supposed to do that."

"Wow, that's ambitious."

"I know. I love his creativity, but when it comes to making those dreams reality... well, that's the hard part." Angela bit her bottom lip. "How can I make a race car that doesn't look tragic?"

"Hmm..." Patrick paused. "I bet some

lightweight wood could work, or possibly a converted wagon of some kind. I could think of some ideas and text them to you."

"Really? That would be amazing." Angela let out a relieved breath. "Would you be willing to help us put the car part of the costume together? I can put together the rest."

"Yeah, I'd be happy to." Patrick chuckled.

"You're such a lifesaver." Angela shook her head, resting an elbow on the desk. "Left to my own devices, I probably would've ended up slapping something together with tape and plastic, and Jake would have had to go trick-or-treating looking like a mangled robot."

Patrick snorted. "I doubt it would have looked that terrible. You should give yourself more credit."

"Um, you saw my attempts at putting together Jake's robot for his school project before. It's a miracle that we got a few pieces together at all." Angela laughed. "You're becoming my go-to person to call when we have crazy projects like this. Sorry to take advantage of your handy talents."

"Don't be sorry." She could hear the smile in his voice, and she fell for him just a little bit harder. "I don't mind at all. In fact, I love it."

CHAPTER THREE

Brooke loved the weekly dinners at her parents' house, especially now that Angela and Jake had moved back to Marigold.

Her folks had started getting more creative with the meals, and they all had lively debates about what to cook every week in their family group text. Brooke always weighed in on the main course ideas, but she had full control over the desserts. Last week, she had gone the simple route with apple pie, but this week she was making a pumpkin pie cheesecake.

She'd come over to her parents' place early to cook the cheesecake, and she peeked into the oven to check on it just as the front door opened. Over the chaos of Jake playing with his grandfather, Mitch, and the music that Brooke's mother Phoebe had put on while she finished up cooking the main meal, Brooke heard Lydia and her boyfriend Grant greet Angela.

Brooke smiled. With all the time the two of them spent at the inn, they had become like family too.

"Hey!" She grinned when Lydia and Grant came in to drop off the salad they had brought, their contribution to the meal. She hugged each of them, peering into the large bowl covered in plastic wrap. "What magic did you guys bring this time?"

"Nothing fancy. Just a kale and cranberry salad. There's cheese too, of course," Lydia said. Her brunette hair was pulled back into a loose ponytail, and her cheeks were just a little pink from the chilly air outside, making her green eyes stand out even more.

"That sounds delicious! A salad without cheese is a sad salad in my world." Brooke waggled her eyebrows, and they all laughed.

"What's for dessert? Everything in here smells incredible." Grant rested a hand on Lydia's back and leaned over to try to peek inside the oven.

"Pumpkin pie cheesecake." Brooke flipped on the light inside the oven to show them. "I tested it out the other day, and it came out well."

"We can have dessert first, right? We're adults,"

Lydia said, grinning up at Grant. He smiled back, his eyes crinkling a bit at the corners. He was a little older than Lydia at forty years old, and Brooke's first impression of him had been that he was a bit of a curmudgeon—but Lydia seemed to have softened him up a bit.

"Yes! Dessert first!" Jake cheered in agreement, skidding to a stop in the doorway to the kitchen.

Brooke laughed. "We can have dessert first when you come over to visit me for lunch one day, Jake. How about that?"

"Yay! And we can play with Scratch?" The little boy had fallen in love with Brooke's kitten and asked to come over at least three times a week to play.

"Of course we can. He misses you."

"I miss him, too," Jake said with a heavy sigh, as if he hadn't seen Scratch in months instead of just three days.

He ran off, sliding across the floor in his Halloween-themed socks, as Brooke took the cheesecake out of the oven and Lydia and Grant helped Phoebe take everything to the table.

Tonight Phoebe had cooked roast chicken with a white wine mustard sauce, one of her specialties, along with roasted Brussels sprouts mixed with bits of pancetta. Mitch had handled the butternut squash mash, and Brooke had baked some rolls. Ever since Phoebe's health scare over the past summer, the whole family had gotten on board with the changes she'd made to her diet and lifestyle. Luckily, Phoebe was a great cook, so her hypotension diagnosis didn't stop them from having delicious food.

Once all the food was out and everyone was seated, Brooke glanced around.

"Where's the wine?" she asked.

"It's here," Travis said, walking through the front door. "And so am I. Sorry I'm late, everyone."

"No problem. We're just glad you could make it." Phoebe welcomed her son in with a wave.

Everyone greeted Travis, who had the bottles of wine in a reusable shopping bag. Even from across the open floor plan of the house, Brooke could tell he was tired. He had taken off his duty belt, but he was still wearing his police uniform, the top buttons undone. Phoebe smoothed his messy hair as he sat down next to her, and he hardly fussed.

Once he was seated, they started plating up their food and pouring the wine. Brooke sighed when she took her first bite of chicken. She'd had her mother's chicken countless times in her life, but she still didn't understand how Phoebe made something as simple as chicken taste so good. The skin was crisp and perfectly salted, and it was juicy even without the sauce. The Brussels sprouts were charred just enough to give them a crunch too, and they were so delicious that even Jake dove into them first.

"How are things at the inn?" Mitch asked once everyone had sated their hunger enough to speak.

"Really great," Lydia said, looking to Angela.

"Yeah, it really is. We decorated for fall the other day, and we've been almost entirely booked for the past several weekends in a row. The reviews keep rolling in after Meredith's amazing review, and some other smaller bloggers have said good things," Angela added, then glanced at Brooke. "And did I tell you that someone tried to smuggle all the pumpkin scones into their bag at breakfast?"

"Seriously?" Brooke laughed. "How did they try to get away with that?"

"Well, she was a pretty bad thief. She just took the whole tray—there were at least six scones left—and tried to walk upstairs with it. When I asked her what she was doing, she said she was just bringing her husband breakfast in bed." Angela shook her head in disbelief. "I offered to wrap up a few for him because we needed the tray. She went bright red and gave them back."

"The pumpkin ones are some of my best."

Brooke beamed, biting her lip. "I've had a pumpkin scone and a coffee with pumpkin spice creamer for breakfast every day this past week."

"That's way too much pumpkin." Travis grimaced, sipping his wine.

"What? Impossible! There's no such thing as *too much* pumpkin in the fall. You have from October to the end of November to eat as much pumpkin spice everything as physically possible." Brooke smirked at her older brother, who hid an amused smile behind his wine glass. "Don't you know that? It's the law."

"Huh. I must have missed that in my police training." Travis playfully rolled his eyes.

"I'm glad to hear that it's all still going so well," Phoebe said. "The inn was a big venture, but I knew you could do it. All of you are getting enough rest, right?"

"Yes. Finally." Angela speared a Brussels sprout with her fork. "Kathy's been a total lifesaver. We've been giving her more responsibilities, and she's learning really quickly."

"I don't even have to drag Lydia away for afternoon walks anymore," Grant said, resting his hand on Lydia's. "With the kinks smoothed out at the inn, it's easier for her to play hooky every once in a while."

The brunette woman's smile turned bashful when Grant looked at her. Brooke's heart melted a little bit. They were adorable together and were so clearly in love. They both deserved it after the grief they had been through.

"How have you been doing, Mom? How do you feel?" Travis asked, cutting into his chicken. He had already cleared half his plate already. "Have you been back to the doctor?"

"I'm feeling great." Phoebe's eyes brightened. "I thought I felt good before my fainting spell, but I realized that I was just going through the motions. I have so much more energy now, and the doctor said my blood pressure looks normal."

"The doc even said it looked like she was fifteen years younger," Mitch added.

"Oh, he was probably just saying that to make me feel good." Phoebe waved off her husband with a laugh. "But if anything, this is making me realize what's really important in life. I was just going and going without taking time to slow down and appreciate what matters most: family and good friends."

Everyone nodded and agreed. Seeing nearly every person she was closest to seated around the table made Brooke realize just how lucky she was too. She knew that she could rely on each and every one of them to have her back whenever she needed it, and she would do the same for them in return.

"Speaking of realizing what's important in life." Phoebe's brows pulled together as she looked over at Travis. "You've been looking so tired lately, honey. You need to slow down. Especially if you want to find a girlfriend like you've said."

Brooke expected her brother to groan and roll his eyes in response, but Travis just shrugged.

"I'm trying. I'm finally on some dating apps and a website." He sipped his wine, looking down at his plate.

"Really?" Brooke perked up. She had been waiting for Travis to take dating seriously for a long time. She knew he wanted to find someone and settle down, but his police training and his work had kept him busy and distracted. "That's so exciting! How's it going?"

He took another drink of wine, then shrugged. "It's okay. It's weird swiping and scrolling around to see if anyone catches my eye. Everyone has four or five sentences about themselves in their bio, and half of them are filled with emojis. I'd rather meet someone the old-fashioned way, but that doesn't feel as easy as it used to. So I might as well give all this a shot."

"A bunch of my friends from high school have met people on dating sites. All it takes is one good date," Brooke said. "You never know when you might make a love connection."

"True. I have a date set for this weekend with a woman I met on one of the better apps. It's more focused on personality than just looks alone, so maybe it'll work out." Travis sighed, sounding exhausted already.

"It'll be great!" Brooke leaned over and nudged him, giving him an enthusiastic smile. "I'm happy for you. It's good that you're getting out there."

Travis just flushed and grinned. Then he narrowed his eyes a little, shooting her a big brotherly look that she knew well. "If we're poking and prodding into everyone's lives, I think it's your turn to take the hot spot. How are the bakery plans coming along? Any new progress?"

Brooke's cheeks flushed this time. "I wasn't poking and prodding! I was just curious!"

"Well, I'm curious too." Travis scooped up another roll from the basket.

Brooke sighed and looked around the table. Every last person here supported her, which calmed her nerves. She had been working at her bakery dream harder than she'd ever worked at anything, and talking to Scratch about all the details wasn't enough—although she loved having him meow back at her regardless of what she said. She needed to open up and share both her successes and setbacks with others, no matter how scary it might be.

"Okay, fair." She took a deep breath. "I've decided it's really time to make a push and turn my dream into a reality if I can. I'm going to do it—I'm going to open up a bakery. I've already filed articles of incorporation as the first step, but I've been working on everything else for a while now."

Everyone's faces lit up at that news, to Brooke's relief. It felt like a small weight had been lifted off her shoulders.

"That's fantastic! What will you name your new business?" Lydia asked.

"It's going to be called Brooke's." She laughed. "Original, I know, but all the other ones didn't seem to click. I feel like it works because it's simple. It's *me*."

"It sounds perfect, sweetheart," Mitch said, beaming with pride. "I know you can do it. But make sure you get insurance for your company, and if you're taking out a loan to get started, you'll want to—"

"Mitch, she's a grownup. I'm sure she's been doing research on all of this and can handle it." Phoebe gently swatted him on the arm, rolling her eyes. Then she turned to Brooke. "We know you'll do great. And we're all here for you if you need any help."

"Especially if you need taste testers," Angela put in with a grin.

Everyone laughed, and Brooke felt a surprising tickle of happy tears at the back of her throat. Her family's support meant the world to her, and she knew she could take on this scary but exciting venture with their help.

* * *

Lydia was stuffed before they even got to dessert, but she made room for some of Brooke's incredible pumpkin pie cheesecake. After the meal ended, everyone stayed seated around the table for a while, relaxing and talking.

She felt full and content, especially with a last glass of wine in her hand. As Angela and Brooke began clearing away dishes, she gave Grant a squeeze on his upper arm and tilted her chin in the direction of the kitchen, a silent signal that she was stepping away. Grant smiled, giving her a small nod before returning to his chat with Mitch and Travis.

In the kitchen, Angela and Brooke were looking at a something on Brooke's phone, sipping their final drinks as well. There was a neat line of Tupperware, filled with leftovers for everyone, stacked on the counter behind them.

"Aw. Scratch is getting so big," Lydia said when she saw what they were looking at. It was an adorable video of the little kitten—although he was much bigger than he had been in the last photos she had seen—chasing a laser pointer.

"He is! He used to climb up my pant legs like it was no big deal, and now I'm like, whoa, hold on." Brooke laughed and put her phone down. "He's still small, though. The vet said he didn't look like he'd be huge or anything when he's all grown up."

Lydia leaned up against the counter, resisting the urge to snag a bite of the last piece of cheesecake on the cake stand behind them. From this angle, she could see Grant chuckling at something Travis said, totally engrossed in his conversation as they sat at the table.

"Hey, since Grant is distracted, can I ask you something?" Lydia asked Brooke.

"Go for it."

"I know you'll be busy getting the bakery off the ground, but if you have time next month, could I commission a cake from you?" Lydia double-checked on her boyfriend over her shoulder, making sure he wasn't eavesdropping and couldn't overhear. "Grant's birthday is coming up in November and I'm planning to throw him a surprise party."

"Oh, how fun!" Angela's face lit up, but she kept her voice low.

"I hope it will be. He told me he hasn't done much for his birthday for the past few years, and I could tell it made him a little sad." Lydia's heart ached, remembering how down he was about it. "I think after Annie's death, some of the fun and magic of his birthday got lost, since there was no one special to help him celebrate. So I want to go all-out and make it a big deal this year."

"That's so sweet!" Brooke beamed. "Of course I'll make the cake."

"Wonderful. Thank you so much." Lydia pulled her into a quick hug.

"What kind of cakes does he like?" When they broke apart, Brooke pulled her phone out again to take notes, her blue eyes shining. "And how many people?"

"I'm not sure about the number of guests yet, but I know he really likes chocolate, the darker the better. But he also likes cherries, so maybe something like German chocolate cake? Grant likes it so much that he put aside his aversion to ice cream without crunchy toppings to try the German chocolate flavor that the Sweet Creamery had a few weeks back."

"He hates ice cream without crunchy toppings?" Angela asked, an eyebrow going up. "So plain chocolate would be a no-go?"

"Exactly." Lydia laughed. "And he loves mint chocolate chunk for some reason."

"Mint chocolate ice cream is kind of like the oatmeal raisin cookie of ice cream—you either love it or you hate it with every cell in your body," Brooke said with a snort.

"Yeah, he's got his quirks." Lydia glanced over at Grant again, warmth filling her chest. He was nodding along to something Travis was saying, looking serious and intense. But when he smiled, it transformed his whole face.

"You guys are absolutely adorable," Angela said with a gentle, happy sigh.

Lydia's cheeks heated up. She'd never thought

she would be described as "adorable" ever again, but sometimes Grant made her feel a lot of things she thought she had left in the rearview mirror.

"Well, so are you and Patrick."

Angela could only smile at that, even though it was absolutely true. Lydia turned to look at Brooke, then Angela did as well.

"What?" Brooke's eyes widened. "*Me?*"

"Yes, you. You asked Travis about his dating life earlier, so now it's all fair game." Angela gently nudged her with an elbow.

"No way. I'm not looking for a relationship right now," Brooke said, shaking her head. "I can't imagine juggling the bakery and a new boyfriend."

Lydia resisted the urge to shrug. Brooke might have said that she wasn't looking, but Lydia was fairly certain that someone had her attention, anyway. She was house-sitting for Hunter, sure, but his name came up an awful lot in conversations, and every time it did, Brooke smiled. He was incredibly handsome, but it felt like Brooke's crush ran deeper than just looks. But Brooke was right—the bakery would probably be her primary focus for a while, and it was sure to take up a lot of time.

The three women got back to tidying up, quickly taking care of the dishes and crumbs from the meal.

Lydia was getting a little tired, so she went to find Grant. He was in the dining room, gathering up the last few glasses and dessert plates. Lydia took some plates off his hands and kissed him on the cheek.

Although he'd been a bit stiff and hard-edged when she'd first met him, he hardly looked surprised at her random acts of affection now. Instead, the corner of his mouth quirked up a little, and his eyes lit up. All the talk of dating reminded Lydia of how lucky she was to have found Grant. His serious, gruff exterior hid a heart of gold, which she never would have discovered if life hadn't pushed them together.

Grant gave her a quick kiss on the forehead before they headed to the kitchen to deposit the dishes, bringing a smile to Lydia's face again. After her husband Paul had passed away more than a year ago, she hadn't been sure she'd ever find someone to love again. She hadn't known if she even *wanted* to.

But Grant couldn't have shown up in her life at a better time.

CHAPTER FOUR

Hunter really admired the costume department's skills—all of the costumes were authentic to the period the film was set in, right down to the stitching and buttons—but sometimes he wished they'd make a few concessions for comfort, especially when it came to sitting. Everything he was wearing made him feel like he was bound like a mummy from neck to ankles. He had kicked off his uncomfortable shoes the moment he got back to his trailer to rest between shots.

He sighed and sat back as much as he could, adjusting his earpiece and balancing his phone on his thigh. His agent, Mimi, was talking his ear off about all of the latest news in the industry. He liked that she cared enough to tell him these things, but hearing all the tiny pieces of gossip that were no big deal in the broader scheme of things made him miss the simplicity and comfort of Marigold.

"Anyway, I've been starting to really focus on your next gig," Mimi said. "I've been fielding some calls about a lot of great potential roles for you. Big ones, too. There's already Oscar buzz about your performance as William."

"Oscar buzz? Really?" Hunter rolled his eyes a little. "Mimi, we haven't even finished shooting the movie yet. How can people be raving about something they haven't seen yet?"

"Well, a lot of people *have* seen you. You aren't exactly filming the movie by yourself, are you?" she pointed out.

"Okay, true, but you know how much goes on between production and the final cut. I could suck in every single scene we've shot. And who knows, I might suck in the ones that are coming up, too."

Mimi just laughed. "Don't be ridiculous. You're too gifted of an actor to give a terrible performance. That's why big names are clamoring for you to audition for some of these new roles."

Hunter drummed his fingers on his knee. Mimi

knew the parts that he was a good fit for, so checking them out wouldn't hurt. "Okay, I'll take a few meetings and do a few auditions while I'm in town."

"Perfect!"

"But I'm not sure if I want another project right away," Hunter added before she could get too excited. "I want to take things slower and focus on the projects that I really want to do instead of picking them just to stay busy."

"All right, then." Mimi sounded a tad unconvinced. "I'll get you those meetings. Keep an eye out in your email inbox."

"Will do. Talk to you soon."

He hung up and sighed. Mimi had been his agent for over ten years, since his early days as an actor, and she had never steered him wrong. But still, he hoped she would be okay with his decision to be choosier about his roles. It meant less of a commission for her, but that was never her motivation anyway—she cared about him as if he were family.

Hunter still had a bit time left before he would be needed on set again, so he called Brooke. It took a few rings, but eventually she picked up.

"Hey, Hunter!" She sounded out of breath.

"Did I catch you at a bad time?"

"No, no. I just got back inside from a run." She laughed. "House sitting for you is totally spoiling me. Between the amazing kitchen and the beachfront running path, I've got everything a girl could dream of. I'm trying to soak it all up while I can."

"You'll always be welcome to jog there if you want, even when I'm back." Hunter smiled, leaning back in his seat. "Oh, and speaking of me being back, there's a short break in production at the end of the month, so I'm planning to come back to Marigold for about a week. It will be a good reset before we head into the last big push of filming."

He missed his new home—missed the quiet atmosphere, the stellar ocean view, and the sounds of gulls on the beach. The film studio had put him up in a very nice space that wasn't too far from where they filmed, and he liked it, but he couldn't find the sense of peace he was after in LA.

"Okay, no problem. I'll clear out and head back to my apartment for that week." Brooke paused, and Hunter heard the water running into a bottle. "Scratch has gotten used to the cozy digs, so he'll probably be a little disappointed to have less space to sprint back and forth and fewer birds to stare at."

Brooke joked around a lot, and she was usually

happy and energetic, so Hunter noticed immediately how flat her words came out in comparison to her usual tone. That wasn't like her. Her positive attitude and easygoing nature were two of his favorite things about her.

"Hey, are you okay?" he asked, standing up so he could stretch his legs. "You sound a little down."

* * *

Brooke shut off the water and blinked, taking a sip from her now-full bottle. She talked to Hunter a lot, but she was still surprised at how perceptive he was, even over the phone. She hadn't thought that she sounded as down as she felt.

She wandered over to the breakfast nook and sat down, sighing. Maybe it was his acting training that made him so good at reading people.

"Yeah, I'm all right. I've just had a rough day." She lifted her hands so Scratch could hop into her lap, kneading her sweatpants with his little paws. "I applied for a small business loan so I could secure that amazing bakery location that I saw the other day, but I wasn't approved. I don't have enough capital to give this a go without it, so I'm kind of at a loss."

"I'm sorry, Brooke. That sucks." Hunter's voice

was soft and made her feel a little better. "If that location doesn't pan out, I'm sure another one will."

"True." Brooke rubbed Scratch's belly when he flipped over onto his back. "I think I put too much hope into it and let myself get attached too soon, assuming the loan would go through. But it didn't, so losing the place hurts even more."

"It's not gone yet," Hunter pointed out. "And there's nothing wrong with getting your hopes up about something you're excited about. It does hurt when you fail, but lowering your expectations for everything and not letting yourself get excited to protect yourself from disappointment is just as bad."

Brooke considered his words, a little weight coming off her shoulders. He was right, and somehow, he had known exactly where her mind was going. She'd been mentally planning on going back to the drawing board and dialing back her goals, just so that the next setback she faced wouldn't hurt as much.

"That's true. Are you a mind reader? Because I would have been lowering my expectations just as we speak if you hadn't called."

"Nope, I'm just a guy who's dealt with a ton of rejection. Getting my start as an actor was rough. I was from a small town kind of like Marigold, so everything was so different in the big city. And my failures were totally embarrassing, too."

Brooke laughed, thinking of the Hunter she knew now. He got nervous before auditions, but he seemed confident in his ability to do his best.

"I can't imagine you totally tanking an audition. It's just not computing." Brooke put her phone on speaker so she could pet Scratch with both hands.

"Oh man, you have no idea." Hunter snorted. "I still cringe thinking about the auditions I had back when I was first starting out. Once, I was auditioning for a TV role—a teen drama—and I went in expecting it to be pretty easy. That was mistake number one, going in with too much confidence. Mistake number two was wearing skinny jeans, which made me feel a little more in character."

Brooke held in a giggle, seeing where his story was starting to go.

"So, I walked in and got tripped up right away. I thought it was just going to be me, the casting director, and maybe the show runner. But it was them, plus other people who had already been cast," he continued. "I dropped my pages, and when I went to pick them up, my pants ripped so loudly that all of LA probably heard it."

Brooke's laughter bubbled over. "Oh my god."

"I know. It was awful." Hunter laughed along with her. "I tried to play it off since they were only going to see my front for the most part, so we kept going. I was so rattled by the pants that I gave one of my worst performances ever. Needless to say, I didn't get the part."

"Okay, that's truly bad. At least I didn't rip my pants at the bank."

"That would have been uncomfortable. And that's only the tip of the iceberg when it comes to awkward auditions." She could hear the smile in Hunter's voice. "But I recovered from my mortification and hopped back on the audition horse. Actually, if I hadn't tanked that audition, I might not have been able to accept the role that launched my career. So it all worked out in the end."

Brooke nodded, even though he couldn't see her. "That's good to know."

"I have to get back to set," he said. "Talk to you later?"

"Yeah, definitely. Bye!"

Brooke hung up, still smiling. Hunter was right. Just because she hadn't gotten approved for the loan didn't mean that it was over. She had fallen a little, but she didn't have to stay down. After all, Hunter had ripped his pants in the middle of an audition and had apparently bombed others, but he was living his dreams now. It was definitely possible.

She hopped up, putting Scratch on the ground, and went to shower feeling a renewed sense of conviction. She could live her dream too, as long as she never gave up.

CHAPTER FIVE

Angela took the race car driver suit that she had ordered online out of its packaging again. Jake had tried it on earlier before they'd come over to Patrick's new house to work on the other parts of his costume. It fit perfectly, but he wanted to sew on some patches and add a stripe to it to match the car. Angela could handle that.

She sat down at Patrick's kitchen table and laid out the patches that Jake wanted to add. Patrick and her son were on the floor, putting together the car. Patrick had helped her find an old wagon at a yard sale, and he was adding lightweight pieces of white wood so Jake could look like he was sitting inside of the race car. It looked great, and she was impressed by Patrick's ingenuity. She would never have thought to use an old wagon that way.

"Okay, let's try this," Patrick said to Jake, stepping back and gesturing toward the car.

The little boy carefully stepped in and sat in the wagon, his eyes lighting up. "Ooh! Does it look cool?"

"It looks really cool," Angela said, smiling. "Is it ready for decoration?"

"Yup, should be." Patrick grabbed the kid-safe paint they had purchased at the craft store and placed it on the newspaper they'd covered the kitchen floor with.

"Can I do it? I want to paint a stripe." Jake tapped the tops of the paints like bongo drums.

"Sure, but let's trace some lines on it first so they'll be straight."

Patrick found a ruler and carefully drew lines where Jake wanted them with a pencil. Then he painted over the lines. Once the lines were set, Jake grabbed a brush and started to paint inside the lines with laser focus. Patrick painted over a patch where the white paint had chipped away at the same time. Seeing them work on the car together made Angela's heart warm.

She adored a lot of things about Patrick, and the

fact that he and Jake got along well was on the top of that list. He wasn't trying to replace her ex-husband Scott, but he was still a positive figure in Jake's life.

Patrick glanced up at her, a smile spreading across his face as he caught her watching them. He stood up, brushing stray bits of wood off his pants as he walked over to her. "What's up? What are you thinking about?"

"Oh, nothing. This just reminds me of shop class back in high school. You were always good at it." Angela gently tugged at the black and red flannel shirt he was wearing. "And you wore shirts like this all the time."

Patrick chuckled, looking down at his shirt. "Oof. Has my fashion really not changed since high school? I'm surprised you even remember that."

"I had a crush on you back then, so I remembered a lot of little details," Angela said. "If you wore a t-shirt for a band I liked, I would freak out about it and think of eighty different ways to talk to you about it. Not that I ever did. I was way too shy to act on it. And then you got together with Aubrey, so it was sort of too late for me to make a move or anything."

Patrick blinked, obviously surprised. "Really? You had a crush on me?"

"Oh, yes. I have pages and pages of cringeworthy diary entries to prove it." She blushed, half grimacing and half smiling. "They're probably at my parents' house, and I need to go burn them some time."

"No! Don't burn them. I bet they're entertaining."

"Oh, they definitely aren't. They're mortifying. At least we're together now, so it's less embarrassing to think about."

Patrick chuckled before leaning down to kiss her softly on the lips, resting his hand on her lower back.

"Life has a funny way of working out the way it's supposed to, doesn't it?"

* * *

The look in Angela's eyes when they broke their kiss made Patrick's heart do a small flip in his chest. He could tell that she was falling for him just as much as he was falling for her.

It felt great and... real.

He hadn't felt like this toward anyone since he and Aubrey started dating in high school, and he was glad he now had the perspective to appreciate how special their connection was.

Life really *did* have a funny way of working out

the way it was supposed to. If Angela had told him how she felt back in high school before Aubrey did, what would have happened? He was glad that nothing had happened back then, as strange as it was to think that.

Despite the ups and downs he'd been through in his love life recently, it felt like everything had worked out just like it was supposed to, and exactly *when* it was supposed to.

His fashion sense might not have changed a lot since high school, but he had. And now he knew that Angela was a much better fit for him than his ex-wife, Aubrey, had been in a lot of ways.

He and Aubrey had had some great years, especially at the beginning when they were riding high on the freedom of starting their adult lives. As it became clear that they were growing apart, they'd tried to keep it together. After all, they had been together since high school and they had been through too much to just let it go.

But he was grateful that Aubrey had been honest about how she felt. If she hadn't, they would have sat for way too long in a marriage that wasn't right for either of them. They had gotten together when they weren't truly sure what they wanted out of life.

Now Patrick could see how fundamentally

different their ideal lives were. She wanted excitement and something new every other day, and he wanted this: making a car for a Halloween costume.

"Wait here for a second. I have something to show you." Patrick squeezed Angela's shoulders and pecked her on the lips again quickly. Then he went into his office to grab the box that had arrived the day before.

Angela eyed him curiously as he returned and put the box on the counter.

"Do you want to be my Halloween date?" Patrick asked, pulling out a magician's hat and a pair of bunny ears. "I was trying to think of a fun costume for a couple, and a magician and his rabbit popped into my head for some reason. I'm up for being either. I figured I'd run the idea by you before I went ahead and got the rest of the costume."

Angela's eyes lit up as she grabbed the top hat. "This is great! I love it. And I love the idea of you dressed up as a gigantic rabbit, walking around Marigold."

"How did I know that you'd pick the magician?" Patrick asked, laughing.

"Because you knew I'd get a good laugh out of the whole thing?"

"Okay, true." Patrick put the hat on her head. It fit perfectly. "So, what do you say? Do you want to do this?"

"Of course I will." Angela played with the rim of the hat, her blue eyes still bright as she waggled her eyebrows at him. "Let's find you a rabbit costume."

CHAPTER SIX

Hunter's t-shirt and jeans felt blissfully loose after changing out of his stiff, heavy period costume.

With a short break scheduled in the filming of *Far and Away*, he was planning to take the opportunity to go back to Marigold for several days. He had his bag packed and ready to go in his trailer since he figured it would be faster to leave straight from the soundstage to head to the airport. As satisfying as his work was, he couldn't wait for a bit of time off.

He couldn't wait to get home.

After checking his reflection to make sure he'd removed the last of the makeup he'd had on for his last scenes, he headed out of his trailer.

"Oh, Hunter! So glad I ran into you," Saffron

said from behind him as he stepped outside. She had also changed out of her costume and into jeans and a t-shirt, with massive sunglasses perched on her face.

"Hey, what's up?" he asked.

"Just wanted to say goodbye before our break." Saffron propped her sunglasses on the top of her head and glanced down at his bags. "Heading home?"

"Yup. I'm going back to Marigold during the break to get away from all this LA madness," Hunter said with a chuckle. "I never thought I'd say it, but I miss the quiet."

"That sounds lovely. I've got a few meetings and some auditions I can't miss, so I'm sticking around." She bit her bottom lip and studied Hunter's face. "Do you want a ride to the airport? I'm happy to drop you off."

"No, but thank you for the offer." Hunter smiled, hoping she wouldn't read into his expression too much. "I called a car, and it should be here any minute."

"Ah, okay. Well, see you when we get back?" She was clearly disappointed, but she managed to mask it at the last second.

"Yeah, see you. Have a nice break."

Hunter nodded at her and walked to the pickup

area, letting out a sigh of relief when he was out of Saffron's earshot. He liked the bubbly actress as a friend, but he knew that if he'd accepted her ride, she would have flirted with him even more. He wasn't in the mood for slightly awkward conversation.

The ride to the airport was fast, at least by LA standards, and the flight went by quickly too. Before he knew it, he was in Massachusetts and getting on the ferry back to Marigold. It was much chillier here than it had been in LA, of course, but the cold was refreshing after the warmth and smog of California.

He spent the entire ferry ride out on the deck, breathing in the salty air.

A cab picked him up a few moments after he reached the island, and he let out a happy sigh as he stepped back into his home, finally feeling like he could relax. It smelled great inside, like vanilla or something sweet, and everything was spotless. Maybe Brooke had been baking—that would account for the wonderful aroma. He walked through the house, checking his plants. They were all thriving. Everything looked exactly as he'd left it.

Once he'd dropped his bag into his bedroom and slipped into some jogging pants and a hoodie, he made his way down the path to his favorite spot on the beach. At this time of year, it was much too cold to dip his toes in, but he liked the sight and the sounds of the water anyway.

He stood on the beach, letting the sounds of the gentle waves relax him even more. This alone was worth moving to Marigold for, in his opinion. There were beaches in California, sure, but finding one even a quarter as peaceful as this one near LA was difficult.

Hunter glanced around, then checked his watch. He wasn't sure if Brooke would be jogging around this time of day or not. Either way, he didn't see her on the sandy beach that stretched out into the distance.

That's too bad, he thought with a twinge of regret.

Then he blinked. What was he thinking? He didn't have to wait to bump into Brooke like he always had before. He had her number, so if he wanted to see her, there was nothing stopping him from making that happen. With a grin stretching across his face, he dug his phone out of his pocket and called her.

"Hey, what's up?" Brooke asked when she answered, her voice as sunny and bright as always.

"Not too much. I just got back home from the airport. Thanks so much for watching everything. It's like I never left." Hunter tucked his free hand into his pocket and wandered down the beach as he spoke.

"Of course, it's no problem at all! Are you jet lagged?"

"I will be, definitely. I don't feel it now since it's still early afternoon, but I'll probably be up watching terrible cooking competition shows at two in the morning."

Brooke laughed. "Well, welcome back regardless."

"Thanks." He smiled, feeling the warmth of her words in his chest. "It's weird to see how much all the decorations have changed since I was here last. It's full-on Halloween season."

"Oh yeah, Marigold goes all out for Halloween. For most holidays, really, but especially Halloween. There will be trick-or-treaters everywhere, and depending on the weather, there's a costume party on the boardwalk every year. And lots of parties, of course, but those aren't really my scene anymore."

"Yeah, I haven't properly celebrated Halloween in ages. Dressing up was fun when I was a kid, but then it became a weird way to one-up people with more elaborate costumes as an adult, at least in LA. You'd think actors would get sick of wearing costumes all the time, but most of them can't pass up an opportunity to dress up. It's almost as competitive as some of the auditions I've gone on."

"That takes the fun out of it," Brooke said. "It's so fun when it's just kids or adults dressing up and goofing around. Or eating candy. My building doesn't really get many trick-or-treaters in comparison to the houses around us, so I usually end up eating all the candy I got for trick-or-treaters all by myself."

Hunter paused, feeling a small twinge of nervousness before he said, "Do you want to come over on Halloween and give out candy with me? If you're free, I mean. I have no idea if a lot of kids will come by, since it's my first fall on the island, but I could use some backup if it gets busy."

"Oh! Sure, that would be a lot of fun," Brooke said. He could hear the smile in her voice. "And hopefully it won't be *too* busy, since I sort of like eating the leftover candy."

Hunter grinned. "I'll buy extra, just in case. See you then."

* * *

Travis sipped his beer, wishing that the couple at a nearby table would finally finish up and pay their check so that he and his date, Gina, could take their place. Ariana, the restaurant Gina had suggested, was packed for the weekend, and they were waiting for their table at the bar. The noise around them only made the intermittent awkward pauses in their conversation even worse.

"So, um..." Gina looked at him, her foot absently jiggling. "I've heard this place is good."

"Yeah, I have too. I've never gotten the chance to try it, so thanks for suggesting it," he said.

"Yeah." Gina smiled, resting a hand on her arm. "I knew that you were the right guy to take here."

Travis smiled politely, even though he felt he was definitely the wrong guy for her in general. He hadn't even finished his drink, but he was already fairly certain this date wasn't going to be one for the history books.

Gina had seemed nice on the dating app they'd connected through. She was pretty, with shoulder-length brown hair and brown eyes, and she worked in marketing. She'd said she was interested in a more serious relationship instead of just a fling, just like he was.

He'd matched with her through whatever

algorithms the app used to pair people up, and he'd struck up a conversation. After being on the app for a little while, he knew that it was a waste of time to message back and forth forever, so he'd asked her out after a few days of chatting through texts.

He was glad he had, because Gina was very different in person than she'd been online. At least he'd found that out sooner rather than later. But now that he knew, he wished he could go home.

She was as pretty in person as she'd been in her picture, but she was trying to win him over in ways that would have been a better bet with someone else. Her makeup was much heavier than it was in any of her photos, and her outfit felt more appropriate for a club than a laid-back dinner. He felt a little out of place next to her in his sweater and dark jeans, although he blended in with everyone else.

"So, you said you moved here recently. Do you have family in the area?" Travis asked, searching desperately for topics to keep the conversation going.

"Um, kinda. I don't really hang out with my family much." Gina sipped her wine. "Not that I hate them or anything, but we aren't going to be having dinners every other week, you know?"

"Right."

Travis nodded, trying not to look as disappointed as he felt.

He was lucky—he loved his family and got along with them well, a privilege that many others didn't have. But he wanted to be with someone who was just as close to her family as he was with his. And eventually, he wanted a close-knit family of his own.

There was another slightly awkward pause, so Travis asked, "And you moved from the suburbs of Boston?"

"Yup."

Travis waited for her to elaborate a little bit, but she just gazed at him expectantly as if waiting for the next question. It was starting to feel like she wanted him to interview her to be his girlfriend instead of having a real conversation. Travis had no idea how to break free of this awkward dynamic, so he sipped his drink and pushed on, just so that the awkward silence wouldn't drown them both.

"Do you like living here? At least so far?"

"Yeah. It's pretty nice. I like the food, and the people are nice. I'm not sure what I'll think in a few years. It would be nice if there were a few more recognizable places, like a Target or a Starbucks or something, so it could feel a little more... familiar, I guess? And normal?" She must have noticed how that sounded, because she quickly added, "Not that the small-town charm is a bad thing, but sometimes I just want to have that big city experience and not have to go all the way back to Boston to get it."

"I get that."

And he did. He sometimes went to the mainland to get things he couldn't find in Marigold, but that wasn't often. Even though there were a lot of small businesses here, they carried a plethora of unique things you couldn't get anywhere else, along with lots of items that you could find at any big box store in the country.

"The businesses here are nice. I've found a couple of really great bars and restaurants." Gina shrugged and glanced at the front podium, where the host was dealing with a line of people. "Kinda slow, though, isn't it? That's another thing—sometimes I just want to speed things up."

Travis wondered why she'd taken a job in a small town if she wasn't a fan of the slower pace, but he held his tongue. Thankfully, a waiter made eye contact with him at that moment and gestured with the menus in his arms.

"Hi, there. Your table is ready," the man said. "If you'll follow me?"

The bar was on the opposite side of the

restaurant from their table, so they weaved their way through the seats and across the waiting area, which was packed. Gina bumped against a woman who was shifting out of the way of another person trying to leave.

"Hey! Watch it," Gina snapped, clutching her wine.

"Sorry," the woman said. Travis got a brief glimpse of her, but he couldn't place where he knew her from right away.

"I almost spilled my wine." Gina frowned in annoyance, as if the incident had been intentional. She shook her head as they kept following the waiter. "God, the nerve of some people."

Travis glanced back over his shoulder briefly to see if he could catch sight of the woman who'd collided with Gina, but she had disappeared into the crowd again. The waiter seated them at a small table in the middle of the restaurant, gave them their menus, and said he'd return shortly to take their orders.

Gina still seemed put out at getting bumped into as she turned her attention to the menu. It all looked good to Travis, so he decided on the halibut in lemon sauce almost right away since it was one of their specialty dishes.

"Gosh, I can't decide," Gina said, sighing. "Do I want to get pasta, or maybe a salad? A salad feels healthier, but it's the weekend. And the dessert is supposed to be amazing... so maybe salad and dessert?"

"The pasta sounds good," Travis said absently, half of his attention on Gina and the other half still trying to pin down where he had seen the woman Gina had bumped into before.

Then it clicked.

It was Jennifer Lowry, the real estate agent Travis had met when she'd called about a break-in at one of the houses she was selling. He hadn't recognized her right away this evening because she was dressed much more casually than she'd been that day, in a pink sweater, jeans, and flats, with her blonde hair in a ponytail. Without her high heels on, she was petite, which made her a little more difficult to recognize, too.

After the waiter took their orders and their menus, Travis excused himself for a moment. Jennifer was still waiting for a table, thankfully, and he found her in the crowd fairly easily.

"Hi. Jennifer, right?" He ducked his head a little to catch her gaze, tucking his hands into his pockets.

"Yeah. And you're Officer Collins, right?" Jennifer smiled.

"Just Travis. I'm off duty." Travis's face warmed, and he was thankful that the restaurant was somewhat dark so she wouldn't notice the redness in his cheeks. "I just wanted to apologize for earlier when you got bumped into. My date was a little rude."

"It's fine, really." Jennifer smiled, brushing off his apology with a wave. "But thank you for saying something. You didn't have to."

"I just wanted to."

Now that Travis said it, he wasn't sure why he'd come over here to say anything at all. He wasn't the one who had bumped into her, but he still felt bad that anyone would snap at someone else over something as small as an accidental bump. Especially someone like Jennifer. Even though they'd only met once, she seemed to be a nice woman.

"That's very sweet." She fiddled with her necklace. It was the same one she'd been wearing the day of the break-in, and he had a sudden memory of her fidgeting with it nervously then too.

Travis smiled, but before he could say anything else, a man called Jennifer's name from near the door. The man waved when he caught her attention, and Jennifer's face lit up as she waved back. He was around Travis's height, with pale brown hair that was cut stylishly and wearing an equally on-trend bomber jacket.

"Oh, I've got to go. It was nice seeing you, Travis. Thanks for saying something, it was really sweet of you." Jennifer gently squeezed his upper arm before heading toward the man who'd called her name.

They greeted each other with a hug, and she kissed the man on the cheek. Travis deflated a little bit. Of course Jennifer would have a date. A nice, beautiful woman with a great career wouldn't stay single for long in Marigold.

He sighed and went back to his table, where Gina was scrolling around on her phone. He hoped the food would come quickly. There was no need to drag the date out any longer than it needed to be, but at least there was a delicious meal to look forward to.

CHAPTER SEVEN

"Trick-or-treat!" Brooke sing-songed when Hunter opened the door to his house, holding up a container filled with Halloween-themed treats in one hand and wine in the other.

She'd decided against a full costume and had only thrown on a pair of cat ears that she had left over from Halloween last year, plus a sweater and leggings. She had always been more excited about the sweets and the cold weather around Halloween than the dressing up.

"I think we're supposed to be the ones handing out the treats, aren't we?" Hunter laughed and stepped aside to let her in.

"True, but that doesn't mean that we can't have some treats ourselves."

Brooke made her way to the kitchen with Hunter behind her. It was nice to be back in his house after a few days away. She had gotten used to the space and —more importantly—the kitchen's high-tech appliances that made baking even more of a pleasure. But she was glad Hunter was back for a few days. She knew that filming took a lot out of him, and he deserved the rest.

"True. It's hard to enjoy a scary movie marathon without something to munch on." Hunter grinned. "What'd you bring?"

"I went with something a little old school, just for nostalgia, and something more grown up." Brooke opened up the container, which had a plastic divider down the middle, and put it on the counter. "Sugar cookies with Reese's Pieces and pumpkin spice blondies. The cookies are a total sugar bomb, of course, but the blondies are much less sweet."

"Wow, these look amazing." Hunter went through one of the drawers and pulled out a corkscrew, then grabbed some stemless glasses. "Did you pick a white wine to go with these?"

Brooke snorted. "Goodness, no. I know nothing about wine."

"I like how your answer was that you don't know anything about wine instead of questioning the idea of wine and cookies together at all." Hunter chuckled and opened the wine, pouring them each a healthy amount.

"See, I told you I know nothing about wine! It didn't even cross my mind to question the idea of the two together." Brooke took her wine. It was a Ladera Sauvignon Blanc, which she had picked up mostly because she'd thought the label was pretty. "Plus, I've spent some evenings watching bad TV and eating cookies with a glass of red. Especially chocolate cookies. I have no shame."

"That does sound pretty good. Anything chocolate and red wine is good in my book." He opened his walk-in pantry. "Maybe we can have some popcorn with the wine first? Otherwise I think I'll plow through everything you've brought in the first hour."

"Sure."

Hunter disappeared for a moment, then came back with a bag of popcorn kernels and a silicone container that Brooke hadn't noticed in the pantry before. He poured the kernels into the container, popped on a lid, and put it in the microwave.

"Oh, how cool," Brooke said, hearing the popcorn starting to pop. "That's a lot less bulky than the big old popcorn maker my parents have."

"Yeah, I got one in some awards show gift basket ages ago. It's much better than the pre-popped stuff in a bag, plus I can try to recreate that movie popcorn experience at home." He smiled. "It feels weird watching a movie without it."

"Yeah, it does."

"When I went to the movies as a kid, I used to buy a bag of popcorn on the way home to eat too," Hunter said.

"That's kind of genius, actually."

Hunter pulled the popcorn out of the microwave, dumped some in a big bowl then tossed it with some butter, parmesan cheese and salt. They nibbled on it while standing at the counter. It was just as good—no, better—than anything Brooke had ever eaten at a movie theater.

"Speaking of movies, how is yours going?" Brooke asked, chasing some popcorn with a sip of wine.

"Pretty well! Everyone gets along, but we have long days." Hunter leaned against the counter. "It's coming together, though, and the cast as a whole has good chemistry. The only downside is the costumes."

"Yeah, you've mentioned how uncomfortable they are. I can't imagine sitting around in that stuff all day in the warmth," Brooke said, shaking her head.

"That reminds me of something that happened the same day that I told you about that horrible audition where I split my pants." Hunter's eyes brightened. "We were shooting this big, dramatic scene where the Duke has to pick some goblets up and make this long speech. The actor playing him dropped one of the goblets mid-scene, but he kept going like it was part of what he was supposed to do. Except when he bent over to pick up the goblet, his pants ripped straight up the back. And loudly, too."

Brooke burst out laughing, nearly choking on some popcorn. "Oh no! Poor guy."

"I know. He laughed it off. But they got it on film, so that makes it a little worse than my horrible audition."

"At least it'll be perfect for a blooper reel."

It took Brooke a few more moments to pull herself back together at the thought, then she remembered how much Hunter's story had helped her feel better after a rough day. He had a way of telling just the right story to make her smile.

"Thank you again for being so supportive and nice that day," she said softly. "It made me feel so much better about not getting the loan."

"Of course. I'd be a pretty bad friend if I didn't say anything," Hunter said, putting down his glass and eyeing the container with the cookies and blondies. "Do you mind if I dig in? These have been staring me in the face for way too long."

"Go for it."

Hunter's hand hovered over the blondies, then the cookies, then back to the blondies. He took one, so Brooke took a cookie. She watched Hunter bite into it as she bit into her cookie, his eyes fluttering closed when he chewed. He was always handsome, but seeing the happiness in his face, even with his eyes closed, made him even more attractive to Brooke.

"These are amazing," Hunter said, taking another bite just moments after he swallowed the first. "I feel sorry for the trick-or-treaters, because this is way better than any of the candy bars we're going to hand out."

"Do you want to try the cookie?" Brooke broke off a piece and offered it to him. "I've made cookies like this before with M&Ms, but never with Reese's Pieces. They felt a little more festive because of the orange and brown, plus they're one of my favorite candies."

Hunter took the cookie and popped it into his

mouth after he swallowed the blondie, giving it a big thumbs up.

"Also amazing. Do you want to sit down in the living room so we can enjoy them and our wine? The trick-or-treaters are probably going to start arriving soon, so we should be closer to the door."

"Sure."

Brooke helped Hunter gather the treats, popcorn, and wine, and brought them over to the living room table. The TV was on, a dark screen paused, and there was a big orange plastic bowl filled to the brim with full-sized candy bars.

"Oh man, if word gets out that you're handing out full-sized candy bars, there'll be kids lining up." Brooke put down the popcorn, then sat down on the couch.

"Luckily we're a little bit out of the way. I'm not sure how fast word spreads amongst kids on the island, but I have more than enough." Hunter sat down next to her, the soft leather cushion pushing them a little closer together. "The only problem is that waves and waves of kids might interrupt our movie. It'll probably take a while for them to get back here, though, so it might not be bad."

Brooke fiddled with her wine glass, trying not to freak out about the inch of space between them. A movie in a semi-dark room, plus wine and treats... it felt a little like a date, just the kind she liked. She liked going out, but sometimes, just watching a movie and eating something delicious was the perfect date for her.

She resisted the urge to fiddle with her hair. *Was this a date?* The idea of it was nerve-wracking—she hadn't been lying at the family dinner when she'd said she was focusing on her bakery—but thrilling.

She definitely had a crush on him, if she was honest with herself. Talking to Hunter on the phone felt great, but talking to him in person was even better. She could see the way his smiles lit up his whole face, and watch how he moved with the ease of someone who knew themselves well, which many men she had dated in the past didn't.

And it didn't hurt that he was the most handsome guy she'd ever known. His dark brown hair and pale gray eyes were still hypnotizing, even after knowing him for a while. But he was also a movie star, and as many late-night conversations with her friends as she'd had over the years, no one had experience with something like this.

"What did you choose?" Brooke finally asked, realizing she had fallen silent for a while.

"It's a surprise." Hunter gave her a half-smile.

"But I promise it's not a slasher film or anything violent. And there are only a few jump scares. And it might be kind of terrible."

"Wait, terrible?" Brooke raised an eyebrow.

"In a very fun way. You know movies that are so bad, they're good? Like that." He reached for the remote. "I watch it almost every year on Halloween. It's really funny and sometimes scary. But mostly funny."

"Okay, I trust you," Brooke said with a chuckle, sitting back in her seat.

"But before we start, I wanted to talk to you about something." He put the remote down on his thigh.

"Sure, what's up?" Brooke asked, thankful she was able to sound cool and collected even as her heart raced.

Was he going to ask her out? Hunter was a really nice guy, the kind of guy who would probably call you to ask you out on an official date, or ask in person if he could. Maybe this evening was a pre-date or something. Was that even a thing? Brooke desperately hoped it was a thing.

"I want to invest in your bakery," he said. "I know you didn't get the loan, but the bank doesn't know how amazing your baking is. I believe in your vision for it. And selfishly, I would love to be able to drop in to get something delicious whenever I'm in town."

Brooke hoped her slight disappointment didn't show. Maybe he didn't feel the same way toward her as she felt toward him. But then, his words actually got through to her.

"Wait... what?" Brooke said, grabbing his forearm. "You want to invest in my bakery? Are you serious?"

"Yeah, I'm dead serious." Hunter smiled, his eyes sparkling in amusement.

"Oh my gosh. Hunter, that's amazing. I... I don't know how I could ever thank you for something like that."

If she hadn't been sitting down already, she would have collapsed onto the couch in shock. Her knees even felt weak.

"Well, you could accept it if you want my investment," Hunter said with a laugh.

"I'd love that, thank you!" Brooke couldn't help herself—she threw her arms around him and gave him a hug. "I'll have to get you all my financial stuff. It's on my laptop at home... should I go get it? What about the trick-or-treaters?"

Hunter let her go and squeezed her shoulders,

still smiling. "Brooke, it's okay. We don't have to dive into spreadsheets and financial statements right now. Let's enjoy the night and have a toast with some cookies."

He split a cookie in half and handed her one side.

"To the bakery?" he suggested, raising his cookie.

"To the bakery." Brooke tapped her cookie against his and took a bite. She couldn't stop smiling, even as she chewed.

CHAPTER EIGHT

"I'm really glad it's chilly tonight. This costume would be brutal if it were warmer," Patrick said, holding Angela's hand as they made their way toward another house on their trick-or-treating journey.

As he'd promised, he was wearing a white rabbit costume. It was loose and made of breathable cotton, which Angela was thankful for. She was worried that she had doomed him to a mascot costume by choosing to be the magician, but Patrick seemed comfortable. Well, as comfortable as an adult could be dressed as a gigantic rabbit.

Angela had on her magician's top hat with a white button-down under a lightweight coat, plus black pants. Since the costume was simple, she was wearing a little more makeup than she wore day-to-day—a bright red lipstick and some smoky eyeshadow. Her blonde hair was tied back in a bun.

She squeezed Jake's hand as he quickly pulled them to the next house. He had his race car driver's helmet on with the visor open, and he was pulling the wagon car that Patrick had helped him build. It was light enough to not be a burden to carry, but still, Patrick held on to the rapidly growing pillowcase filled with candy with his free hand.

The neighborhood was bright with decorated houses, and the streets were filled with kids and their parents trick-or-treating. It was lovely to see. Back in Philadelphia, kids went trick-or-treating too, but it didn't feel as fun and communal as this did. She passed by people wearing face paint and realized that she knew them from the antique store she loved, and waved to old family friends.

Angela was glad that Patrick was so game to go trick-or-treating, even though he likely hadn't gone since he was a kid himself. He was already fitting into her and Jake's lives easily.

"Trick-or-treat!" Jake said the second the door to the next house opened.

"Wow, what a costume!" the woman who answered the door said. She was wearing a pair of cat ears with a black t-shirt and Halloween print pajama bottoms. "Cool race car!"

"Thanks!" Jake beamed, showing off the space where his tooth had fallen out two days before.

He grabbed some sour gummy candy from the woman's bucket of candy and stuffed it into the bag. After saying another thank you, they were off to the next houses. Each time, Jake got compliments on his costume, and the smile didn't leave his face. He skipped a few feet ahead of Angela and Patrick once they reached a street that was closed off to traffic.

"I'm not sure how you'll outdo yourself next Halloween. You have a knack for creating costumes," Angela said to Patrick, bumping her shoulder against his.

"I'm up for the challenge." He grinned. "Though I don't even know what Jake could ask for that could be more over the top."

"Now that you've said that, he'll probably find just the thing." Angela laughed. "Probably like a space shuttle or something."

"I think I could tackle it." Patrick laced his fingers between hers. "If not, there's always the internet."

They walked in comfortable silence behind Jake, gathering more and more candy, until a man wearing a zebra costume waved from across the street. Patrick waved back at the man, who was with his wife and a little boy who was around Jake's age, and walked up to them.

"They're some old neighbors of mine," Patrick explained. Angela nodded. "Hey, how are you guys?"

"We're good!" The woman, who was dressed like a tiger, smiled brightly. "Long time, no see. We almost didn't recognize you with that costume on."

Patrick laughed. "Yeah, it's been too long. This is my girlfriend, Angela. Angela, this is David, Cassidy, and their son Will."

"Nice to meet you all," Angela said, shaking everyone's hands.

Jake and Will eyed each other's costumes, almost curiously. Will was dressed as Spider-Man, who Jake was a fan of. Angela watched them out of the corner of her eye as Patrick caught up with his friends. Angela didn't recognize Will from Jake's class, so it didn't seem like they would know each other well. Jake was rarely ever shy, though, so that didn't seem to stop him from talking about candy and Spider-Man.

As sociable as Jake was, Angela still got worried about him meeting new kids. Other children could be harsh, and her protective instincts were strong. But at the same time, she knew that she had to let him struggle from time to time, or he wouldn't grow.

Angela chuckled along with Patrick at one of David's jokes until her attention was abruptly brought back to the kids.

"Nobody likes race cars," Will said, smacking Jake's car. "They're for babies."

"They're not!" Jake pushed Will, which made Will push back right away.

The two started to get rougher before the adults got them away from each other.

"Hey! No fighting!" Angela said, pulling Jake away from Will by the hand.

Will's parents pulled him a few feet away and scolded him, and Angela put more space between them. Patrick told them he'd catch them later and stayed close to Angela. She squatted down so she was eye-level with Jake and held him by the shoulders. His face was red, and tears threatened to spill over onto his cheeks.

"Jake, that's not okay. You can't hit people," Angela said, brushing a bit of dirt off his costume.

"But... but he said race cars were for babies, and I'm not a baby." Jake wiped his eyes with the backs of his hands.

"Still, that doesn't make it okay." Angela noticed a red and blue wristband that must have come off Will's costume in the scuffle. "Is this Will's? Did it come off when you two were fighting?"

Jake nodded. "I guess so."

"Okay, let me bring this back to him," Angela said with a sigh, standing up. "Patrick, can you stay with Jake while I return this?"

"Of course," Patrick said, tugging Jake out of the middle of the sidewalk, concern written all over his face.

* * *

Patrick found a strip of sidewalk that was out of the way and sat down on the curb with Jake, helping the little boy take his race car driver helmet off. He was hiccupping and crying, his face red and his fists clenched.

Patrick gently squeezed his shoulder as Jake continued to cry. He completely understood where the angry tears were coming from. It had been a long,

long time since he'd gotten in a fight, but he knew how tough it could be as a young kid. Other kids could be mean without even realizing it, and the feelings that came from being a target could be overwhelming.

His dad had sat him down just like he was sitting with Jake after one particularly bad argument with a friend on a summer evening. Patrick could hardly remember what it had been about—he'd been around twelve or thirteen at the time, and the fight had probably been about video games or something equally unimportant in the big scheme of things.

But Patrick remembered how his dad had helped him understand that sometimes, he just needed to walk away from conflicts and maybe do something more productive to take his mind off it. His father's words clicked with him.

Patrick's father wasn't a literary person by any means, but he'd known that Patrick liked stories. He'd gotten Patrick a nice notebook, and Patrick had started writing down a few stories and ideas. When school had started back up, he'd joined the writing club, and the rest was history. Now he was lucky enough to write novels full time and make a comfortable living doing so.

"What happened?" Patrick asked. "It seemed

like you and Will were getting along just fine for a little while."

"He said that no one liked race cars and that they're for babies, but they're not for babies. And everyone likes race cars," Jake said, resting his hands on his car. "And then I pushed him because he was wrong, and he pushed me back."

Patrick nodded, waiting for Jake's tears to slow down a little bit.

"What he said wasn't very nice, but pushing someone isn't nice either. Hitting people can really hurt," Patrick said, opening the bag of candy and going through it to find Swedish Fish, one of Jake's favorites. "Using your words is a better way to show how you feel because it doesn't hurt anyone. And it's what a grownup would do."

Jake sniffed and accepted the Swedish Fish from Patrick, tearing the packet open and shoving them into his mouth. Patrick waited for Jake to chew, briefly worrying about any loose baby teeth he might have, but Jake didn't seem to have any trouble.

"But I already pushed him," Jake finally said, his voice filled with despair. "I already hurt him."

"You can always apologize, even if the other person doesn't," Patrick said quickly, before Jake could burst into tears again. "Everyone makes mistakes."

"Even grownups?"

"Especially grownups." Patrick chuckled.

"It doesn't seem like it."

"They do. Even very old people make mistakes sometimes because we're all always learning," Patrick said.

"I guess," Jake mumbled. "But what do I do? I feel real mad still."

"You don't have to stay mad at someone forever—sometimes it's better to let things go."

Jake's small shoulders sagged in defeat, and he didn't say anything for a while. He finished his packet of candy and Patrick took the wrapper, crumpling it and tucking it back in the bag to toss later. Patrick wasn't sure if he had gotten through to Jake at first, but soon, the boy nodded.

"I want to say sorry to Will," Jake finally said.

"You do? That would be very nice." Patrick stood up and Jake followed suit.

They walked over to where Angela was still speaking with David and Cassidy, who stopped talking when they saw Jake.

"Um, I just wanted to say I'm sorry for pushing

you," Jake said quickly, his cheeks flushed. "It wasn't nice."

Cassidy gently nudged Will.

"I'm sorry I said a mean thing and pushed you too," Will said, looking at his feet. "I like the stripe on your helmet."

"I like your web-shooter," Jake said, smiling.

Both boys grinned, sniffling a little, and Patrick's shoulders relaxed, as did Angela's. She glanced at him over her shoulder, the lines of stress on her features replaced with a grateful smile.

The boys started talking about Spider-Man again, and the tension in the air disappeared. The two little kids got excited about trick-or-treating again, and everyone started walking to the next house together. Jake and Will's conversation shifted to candy soon after, discovering that they both loved anything chewy, and the two of them compared missing teeth.

Angela caught Patrick's hand and laced her fingers with his, pulling him down and giving him a kiss on the cheek.

"Thank you for talking to Jake," she said. "I'm really glad he has you in his life."

Patrick's cheeks flushed. Thankfully, it was too dark out for it to be obvious, especially since they weren't under a street lamp, but it wasn't so dark that she couldn't see his smile.

"He's a good kid with a good heart." He squeezed her hand, watching Jake and Will frantically ring the doorbell of the next house. "I'm glad to be in your lives, too."

CHAPTER NINE

Brooke tugged her fleece jacket tightly around her body, feeling glad that she had chosen it over a lighter jacket when the wind cut across the water. She and Angela had continued their morning walks, even as the weather cooled, and it was just warm enough to still be able to enjoy the outdoors.

As much as Brooke loved the beach in the summer, the beach in the winter had its own charm. Everything seemed to have a frosty tinge to it, and there were hardly any people there. Its calm was just what she needed as a break from her busy life.

"How was Halloween with Hunter?" Angela asked, winding her scarf around her neck so the wind wouldn't blow it away. "What did you guys do?"

"It was great! We handed out candy, of course, which the kids loved. He had full-sized bars."

"Ooh, I bet Jake would have loved that."

"I know. I should have texted you guys to let you know, but we were swamped for a bit. I brought home some leftover bars that I can give him when he comes over next time. They all came in big waves. But when we had a moment, we watched this hilariously bad horror movie while eating some cookies and blondies," Brooke said with a smile, remembering how hard they'd both laughed at the movie's absurd plot.

Hunter hadn't been kidding when he'd said it was amazing for all the wrong reasons. She liked how goofy he could be—it was the last trait she'd expected him to have when she'd first met him. She found it oddly adorable when his eyes lit up and he laughed at something silly.

"That sounds nice and relaxing."

"Yeah, it was. And even better, he offered to invest in my bakery." Brooke's smile broadened. "He believes in it that much."

"What? Brooke, you need to start with news like that!" Angela grabbed Brooke's arm. "That's amazing news!"

"Thank you! It's been such a rollercoaster. I told him how disappointed I was in not getting the loan and he made me feel so much better about it. Then he offered me the help, and I'm back on a high again." Brooke's smile faded a little, thinking about her slight disappointment when she'd realized he wasn't asking her out. "But I feel a little conflicted, too."

"I can see that all over your face," Angela said, tucking her hands deeper into her pockets. "Why?"

"I have feelings for him, I think." Brooke's cheeks, which were a little flushed from the cold, warmed as she blushed for an entirely new reason. Angela nodded in her peripheral vision, and Brooke was relieved that her sister didn't say *I knew it*. "And we're good friends. He said he believed in the bakery, but I don't want to be a charity case or anything."

"You aren't a charity case, Brooke! Even though Hunter has a lot of money, he wouldn't invest in something he doesn't believe in." Angela squeezed Brooke's arm again. "And you know how much he loves your baking."

"True." Brooke sighed. She knew Angela was right even if it was hard to banish her fears. Their friendship was an unlikely one from the outside, so this gesture of his felt even more unexpected—a small-town girl and a Hollywood movie star going into business together.

"Trust me, it's a good thing. Having an investor will help your dream come to life so much sooner."

"Also true," Brooke said. "He's back in LA finishing up the film shoot for the next month, but we've already drawn up the contract and he wrote me the check. I can start making moves. I have a space in mind and everything."

"That's so great! It's finally happening." Angela ran her hand down Brooke's arm and gave her cold fingers a squeeze, making Brooke smile.

"I know. It's feeling closer and closer every day."

And that was the important thing—the more exciting thing. A year ago, she wouldn't have dreamed of being this close to opening her own bakery, but now she had money for a space, more experience baking huge batches for a crowd, and more knowledge about how to run a business.

Even though part of her still wished Hunter had asked her out, she was glad that he believed in her enough to invest in the bakery. She cared about her love life, but she knew that fulfilling her dream would be much more satisfying in the long run, whether she was in a relationship or not. Dating could wait.

"Where's the space that you had in mind?" Angela asked.

"It's *perfect*," Brooke said with a dreamy sigh. "It's on a busy strip downtown, not too far from the Sweet Creamery, and it has this gigantic window in the front. I can imagine putting in some displays of treats or maybe a cool sign. There's plenty of space for big, cozy chairs, and hopefully there'll be enough outlets for people to come work and hang out. There's already a commercial kitchen in there, too."

"What about the interior design?" Angela's smile broadened. "Do you need help with it?"

Brooke laughed. "Of course I've thought about the design, though all I know is that I can see it being pink or coral."

"I've never designed a bakery before," Angela said, looking off into the distance as if she were imagining the bakery as Brooke described it. "But I'm excited to help you out. Pink or coral and cozy sounds like a great place to start."

"Or maybe pink *and* coral?"

"That could definitely work too."

"And big, cozy chairs are a definite must. I'm

thinking it will be the kind of place where people will hang out and work."

"Ooh, I'm already seeing color schemes," Angela murmured, her eyes brightening. "Maybe different shades of pink, coral, and mauve..."

Brooke glanced at her older sister as they turned back toward the Beachside Inn. Angela looked just as excited as she felt herself. Angela had inspired Brooke so much, and Brooke had loved being part of her sibling's journey to open the inn. Now Angela could help her with pursuing her own dream.

She had never imagined them taking this path in life, but it felt like the perfect fit.

* * *

Since Kathy was tending to the front desk, Lydia took a moment to check her email, finding another RSVP for Grant's surprise party in her inbox. Perfect. The guest list was growing longer and longer, even as the date of the party rapidly approached. She put down the person's name on the "yes" list she kept in a separate file and looked over the other plans she had made.

There were going to be a lot of guests, but the

party itself was going to be low key. There was going to be cake, of course, and some other finger food. They were going to decorate the inn for the occasion as well. She just had to figure out how to coordinate the party space and the guests going in and out. Thankfully Kathy was going to be working that day, so she could help keep the lobby empty long enough for everyone to surprise Grant.

Grant had no idea that the party was happening, or so she hoped. He was fairly stoic, so sometimes it was hard to tell whether he thought something was up or not. The party was happening this coming weekend, so they only had to keep the secret a little longer.

She was excited to give back to him, and to make his birthday feel like a special day. He'd helped her find herself again, and she hadn't felt this young and full of life in a long time. Waking up every day with a pep in her step, looking forward to going out in the world, was a feeling she never wanted to let go of again. Giving him a fun party was a small way she could show him her love and gratitude.

Lydia nibbled on a muffin, then swept the crumbs off her fingers, switching over to her plans for the food. Brooke was making the cake, but they were also planning on having finger foods that Grant liked from the place that had catered the inn's opening party. They had gone to a number of Marigold's amazing restaurants, so she had a good idea of what he'd pick on his big day.

In the distance, she heard Angela and Brooke cheerfully greet Kathy at the front desk and then head back toward the office.

"Hey, how was your walk?" Lydia asked when the two came into the office.

"Good! We talked about the bakery and caught up. It's getting cold out there, but it's not unbearable yet." Angela unwound her scarf from around her neck and hung it up. "What are you up to? Kathy's got everything under control?"

"Yup, as always. I'm working on Grant's party. The last few RSVPs are coming in." Lydia stretched. "I'm not sure if my body feels tense because I'm excited to surprise him or if it's all these details driving me crazy."

"I'm sure it'll come together perfectly." Brooke said, taking off her coat. "What details do you need help with?"

"I'm not sure. I think I just have to make sure everything's here on time," Lydia said. "I want it to go off without a hitch."

"Grant will love it no matter what," Angela pointed out. "And he'll be so surprised. He has no idea you're planning this."

"You think he's still completely in the dark about it?" Lydia asked. "I told him I was planning on taking him to dinner that night, but I'm worried I sounded weird."

"He definitely has no idea." Brooke laughed. "When he stopped by to pick you up for lunch the other day, he mentioned to me how excited he was to try the restaurant you're supposedly taking him to for his birthday, so I don't think he's caught on."

"But what if he's just pretending not to know anything?" Lydia bit her bottom lip.

"I doubt he'd do that. I really don't think he suspects a thing and everything's already coming together," Angela said.

"Speaking of things coming together..." Brooke waggled her eyebrows excitedly. "I've made up my mind about the cake."

"What are you making?" Lydia's mouth started to water before Brooke even answered. Brooke's cakes were just as good as everything else she baked, but it had been a while since Lydia had eaten any of her pastries besides what she made for breakfast at the inn.

"Triple chocolate with a bit of cherry—chocolate cake with chocolate buttercream, crunchy chocolate candies, and cherry compote between each layer, all topped with chocolate ganache." Brooke grinned. "So it's sort of like a German chocolate cake, but with a twist."

"That sounds beyond amazing," Angela said, looking just as hungry as Lydia felt. "I can't wait, and it's not even a cake for me."

"Don't deliver the cake early or we'll all plow through the thing before Grant can even see it." Lydia snorted, the comical image of them trying to hide the evidence of the half-eaten cake from the guests popping into her head.

"That's the struggle I go through every time I bake something for someone else." Brooke grinned. "I've even thought about making extra batter for a few cupcakes to avoid temptation in the past, but I haven't done it yet."

"Oh, that's a good idea," Lydia said. The thought of Grant's cake in cupcake form sounded equally appealing. "Are you going to do that for Grant's cake?"

"If you want me to, sure. It sounds like we'll need them to help the cake last until the party." Brooke checked her watch. "Speaking of baking, I've got to get to the kitchen to start prepping for tomorrow."

She finished peeling off her outside layers and headed to the kitchen, leaving Angela and Lydia in the office. Brooke's efficiency in making everything for the inn was still impressive, even after all these months.

"What time do you need us here to decorate on the day of the party?" Angela asked, sitting down across from Lydia.

"Maybe an hour and a half before, to be safe? It shouldn't be too hard since the inn will already be tidy." Lydia checked her running to-do list for the celebration. "And Grant's not big on decorations, really. His house is kind of a bachelor pad, but clean —he has two paintings of boats in two different rooms, but that's about it on the décor front. But it would be weird to not have anything decorative, so I got some streamers and might get balloons. I hope it looks nice."

"He'll love anything you put up. He adores you," Angela said, waving her hand as if to clear Lydia's worries from the air.

"I hope so. I'm excited." Lydia bit her bottom lip as she noticed a message alert pop up at the corner of her screen. "Ah, it's Kathy. She's going on her break. We should get down to business."

"Let's do it."

They went over the inn's to-do list and split up to take care of things. Lydia bubbled with excitement all day long. She just hoped she could keep it all a secret from Grant for one more week.

CHAPTER TEN

Grant sighed, watching his crew load up the last of their gear from their final job of the day. Even though he had mostly gone with his crew to their various landscaping jobs to oversee the work instead of getting in there like he used to, he was tired.

Maybe it was age, or maybe it was just his mood. He loved his business and his work, but he'd been dragging his feet all day and grumbling to himself. He thought of himself as a fair boss, but his team knew that he could be cranky at times. Still, they were good guys who showed up and worked hard for him no matter what.

"Happy birthday, boss," one of his newer employees, Eugene, said as he hopped into a car with a few other guys.

"Yeah, happy birthday. Go eat some cake or something," Tim, another employee of his landscaping company, said with a grin.

"Thanks, guys. See you tomorrow." Grant nodded in their direction, then headed over to his car.

He really wanted cake, or anything to eat. He was hungry, which was only making his grumpiness worse. He had scarfed down half a sandwich in five minutes around noon, and it was getting close to six now. He had thought about taking the day off for his birthday, but had decided against it at the last minute. A lot of clients wanted to winterize their lawns, and there were several new guys on the crew who probably needed supervision, so it wasn't a good idea to stay home.

He waited next to his car while the last few employees checked in with him on their way out, then hopped into the vehicle. Luckily, he only had a bit of dirt on his boots, and he was wearing his nice work shirt that he wore when he had meetings with clients—he was going straight to the restaurant to meet Lydia for his birthday dinner.

The thought of Lydia put a smile on his face, the first one he'd worn all day. Once he saw her, he knew he'd feel better. He always did. Her warm smile, sense of humor, and thoughtfulness made him fall in love with her more every day.

His phone buzzed on the front seat of his truck, and he saw that it was Lydia.

"Hello?" Grant said when he picked up.

"Hey, honey. How are you?"

"Eh, not bad." Grant drummed his fingers on the steering wheel. "Tired and ready to eat. How about you?"

"About the same. I'm excited to see you." He could hear the smile in Lydia's voice, and it lightened his mood a little. "But can I ask you something? Are you on your way to the restaurant?"

"Yup, I'm about fifteen minutes away. What's up?" He rolled to a stop at a light.

"Great. Would you mind doing me a favor? Could you pick something up for me really quickly at the inn? I forgot it." She sighed. "It'll be fast, I promise. It's just on the front desk where I left it in a blue bag. You won't be able to miss it. And don't open it, even though it's not your gift."

He ran a hand over his face then pinched the bridge of his nose. His stomach was growling, and he just wanted to sit down with a glass of wine and some bread to take the edge off his hunger. But Lydia rarely ever asked for favors, and she rarely ever forgot anything. It must have been important.

"Yeah, I can," he said. "I'll be another five minutes, then."

"Thanks, see you soon. Love you."

"Love you too."

He hung up and sighed. It was just a quick favor, but making one extra stop wasn't helping him feel less cranky. He took a left turn instead of a right turn, heading toward the Beachside Inn. He parked in the little lot and headed up the front steps. Now that the inn was open, he was used to a certain level of hustle and bustle around the place, even on the weekends, but it was a little quiet today.

He opened the front door, expecting to see Kathy or Angela at the front desk, but instead, it was empty.

Suddenly, people jumped out from behind the desk and from the other rooms.

"Surprise!" they shouted.

Grant blinked, taking a step back. He was so shocked that it took him a moment to process what was going on. The only other time the inn had been this full was when Angela and Lydia had thrown the grand opening party.

He took in all the faces smiling at him, from Kathy to Lydia's aunt Millie to Eugene and Tim, who had changed from their work shirts into different t-shirts. All of his friends were there, even ones he hadn't seen in a while.

Then it clicked—they were all there for him. And he knew exactly who had invited them. Who had made all of this happen.

Lydia slipped around Tim and Eugene, a shy smile on her face. She was wearing a teal blue sweater dress that he had complimented her on a week ago, and she still looked just as beautiful in it today. Grant put his hand to his chest in mock surprise. Of course Lydia had put together this whole thing. In some ways, he thought he shouldn't have been surprised at all. A simple dinner was a lovely gesture, but Lydia always went above and beyond.

He grinned and pulled her in for a hug, then a kiss on the lips. She smiled into the kiss and squeezed his upper arms as she pulled back.

"Happy birthday!" someone shouted from the back, which everyone else echoed.

"Wow, thank you, guys," Grant said, a genuine smile warming his face.

"There's food in here," Lydia said, pulling him toward one of the common rooms where most of the people were milling around. "I know you must be starving."

The massive table was loaded up with all of his favorites, from mini crab cakes to bacon-wrapped shrimp. It was like Lydia had been taking note of every single food he loved in their time together and put it all on a table. The decorations were his favorite shade of green, brightening up the room even more. He loved how attentive she was to what he liked.

A path cleared between the table and the back, revealing Brooke and Travis carrying a huge, three-tiered chocolate cake. Everyone *ooh*'d and *ahh'd* at it as they put it on the table. It looked incredible, and had *Happy Birthday Grant* written on it in red letters, with two candles in the shape of a four and a one.

"Oh, we need a lighter!" Brooke said, throwing her hands in the air with a slight sigh. "How do I always forget it?"

Everyone chuckled as she went back into the kitchen to find a lighter for the candles.

Grant turned to Lydia, who was beaming up at him. He slid his arm around her waist and pulled her closer.

"I'm glad you guys went with the number candles instead of forty-one individual candles,"

Grant murmured. "We wouldn't want to burn the whole place down."

"Oh, stop," Lydia said, playfully smacking him on the arm and laughing. "Forty-one isn't that old."

"I guess not." Grant shrugged. He didn't feel forty-one, though that was partially because of Lydia. Being around her made him feel young again in the best way. "I'm so surprised that you pulled this off. This is amazing. I don't think I've ever had a birthday party this big before."

"I'm surprised you didn't catch on. Keeping a secret from you is so hard."

"Now that I think about it in retrospect, I should have known something was up," Grant said with a laugh. "You never forget anything, and you sounded a little nervous when you asked about dinner."

"Oh no, now I won't be able to pull off another surprise!" Lydia laughed too, then grinned. "But glad I was able to do it at the same time. I like to make a big deal out of life's little moments, so you'll have to get used to this as long as we're together."

Grant smiled and kissed her on the forehead. "I think I can manage that. Thank you, sweetheart."

* * *

Lydia was so happy that her heart felt like it might burst.

After Brooke lit the candles, everyone sang Happy Birthday to Grant. He blew the candles out easily, and then they cut the cake. Everyone was eyeing it, even with all the delicious food spread out on the table near it. Grant got the first slice and Lydia watched him take a bite, his face lighting up.

"Are there little crunchy candies in this?" he asked after taking another huge bite. "And cherry?"

"Yup. It was all Brooke's idea, but I told her about your aversion to smooth ice cream. I figured that would apply to other sweets too." Lydia served herself a slice and dug in too, letting out a quiet groan of pleasure. "This is so delicious."

"I think it's the best birthday cake I've ever had in my life," Grant said, his mouth slightly full. "Thank you, Brooke."

"No problem! I'm glad you love it." Brooke grinned, grabbing a little plate. "I'm excited to finally try it."

Lydia laughed as Brooke enjoyed the cake she'd baked, doing a little happy dance when she took a bite.

The party kicked into full swing once more people had tried and fallen in love with the cake.

Quiet music played through the speakers they had set up, some of Grant's favorite songs, which floated over the sounds of laughter and warm conversation. Lydia drifted around the room with Grant, who greeted his friends and employees. She was so glad she had invited as many people as she could. Grant wasn't the bubbliest person, but he was kind and loyal to everyone he knew. Being around his friends brought out his soft side.

Eventually, Lydia drifted into the kitchen, letting Grant catch up with everyone he hadn't seen in a long time. Angela was there with a now-empty platter of crab cakes.

"The party is going so well!" Angela said, raising her hand to high-five Lydia.

"It is!" Lydia clapped her hand against her friend's. "I swear he was going to catch on when I told him to come to the inn and pick something up for me. He paused for a second on the phone, and I thought it was over, but he was just having a rough day."

He had sounded so down that it hurt Lydia's heart to think about it. He'd sounded frustrated at her request, but he'd gone ahead and agreed anyway, thank goodness. She was lucky that he was the kind of man who would go out of his way for her.

Otherwise, the party might not have gone off as well as it had.

"Can you help me with the rest of these crab cakes?" Angela asked.

"Of course."

Lydia grabbed one small tray, and Angela grabbed the other before they both headed back out to the party. They dropped off the food and reloaded their plates before splitting up to find their respective partners. Grant had migrated into the main part of the inn and was talking to one of his employees, chuckling at something the other man had said.

After a few moments, his employee drifted over to the reloaded food table, giving Lydia the perfect chance to wrap Grant in a hug. She inhaled his grassy scent and squeezed him once more before letting go. They stood side by side and looked around at the party, which was still in full swing.

"I'm surprised this many people showed up to a party in my honor. It must have been your charm that got them here," Grant teased.

"Oh, of course. I write a killer party invite," Lydia joked. "But for someone who's a bit of a curmudgeon, there are a lot of people on this island who like and care about you. It's almost as if you have a good heart under there."

"I can see that now." Grant squeezed her waist and kissed her forehead, softly chuckling at her joke. "But there's only one person that I really want to like me."

Lydia chuckled, knowing that she was that person, and leaned into him, looking out over the crowd around them. "You don't have anything to worry about there."

CHAPTER ELEVEN

Scratch had been a scrawny little thing when Brooke had found him outside of her apartment, but his appetite had quickly helped him put on the pounds. Now he meowed loudly for his breakfast, winding himself around Brooke's ankles as she walked.

"Scratch!" She scolded the kitten as she nearly tripped over him, just barely managing to keep her cell phone from flying across the kitchen. Scratch didn't seem to notice or care.

"You okay?" Hunter asked her through the phone, chuckling.

"Yeah, Scratch is just hungry and doesn't seem to understand that even though we live together, I don't have his cat-like reflexes." Brooke cradled the phone between her shoulder and her ear, then grabbed a can of wet cat food. Scratch meowed again, trotting over to his food bowl. "He's acting like he hasn't eaten in days."

"I think I heard him meowing. Or was I imagining things?"

"Yup, that was him. He has a real set of lungs on him. Plus, your kitchen is echoey." Brooke shook the food into his bowl, and he dove in face-first. "Now that he's eating, I can walk safely. Good thing, too, because I'm going to check out the space for the bakery today, and I'd rather not end up in the hospital first."

"Yeah, that would be pretty unfortunate," Hunter said. "What time are you going?"

"In about twenty minutes. It's about ten minutes from here." Brooke let out a heavy breath. "This is your last chance to back out on the investing thing."

Hunter laughed. "Nope, I'm not backing out. I'm all in."

"Okay, then here's *another* chance to back out." Brooke grinned, heading to the bathroom to do her hair. Hunter paused. "So you're backing out now?"

"Still no, Brooke," Hunter said. "The only thing that could make me back out is if you suddenly decided to stop baking things with sugar. And even then, I'd have to think about it."

Brooke put her phone on speaker and put it on the bathroom counter. "Yeah, that's never going to happen. I'll make things with bananas or applesauce as sweeteners if I have to, but nothing beats the real deal."

"So I'm still all in."

Brooke brushed her damp hair for a few moments, letting his words sink in. She knew that they were both joking around, but Hunter wasn't lying. He was really in this with her.

"Thank you again, Hunter," Brooke said softly, quickly putting her hair into a braid. "This investment is everything to me. It's letting me actually move forward with my dream, and I'm really grateful."

"Well, I believe in the business," Hunter said, his voice equally soft. "And I believe in you, more importantly."

Brooke smiled, warmth filling her chest as she looked herself over in the mirror. She was wearing her favorite dark blue sweater and her nicest jeans since seeing the space was a casual event. Besides, she could see herself as the type of business owner to not fuss too much over being too formal. It was an easy image to conjure since she believed in herself just as much as Hunter did.

"Thank you, Hunter."

"You'll do great today, I know it. Go get 'em," he said. "I've got to get back to set. Let me know how it goes."

"I will. Good luck on your shoot today!"

They hung up, and Brooke gave herself one more smile in the mirror. Hunter's mini pep talk gave her a new wave of confidence, which she carried with her as she drove over to the space. It was just as perfect as she remembered, and now that she was stepping inside, it was even more so. It smelled clean, but Brooke could easily imagine how it would feel to walk in and smell freshly baked cookies.

Jennifer Lowry, her real estate agent, was already inside, standing at what Brooke envisioned as the check-out area with a tablet in her hands. Unlike Brooke, she was more dressed up in heeled boots, a sweater dress, and tights, her blonde hair down around her shoulders. Despite the difference in their outfits, Jennifer's smile made Brooke feel at ease right away.

"Good morning!" Jennifer said, extending her hand to Brooke. "It's nice to see you in person!"

"It's nice to meet you in person too!" Brooke shook her hand and looked around. "Wow, this looks great!"

"Isn't it adorable? Let me show you around." Jennifer put her tablet down on the counter. "Let's start in the back."

Brooke couldn't keep her gaze from devouring every detail in the space, from the built-in shelves along one back wall to the tiling near the bathroom that was nicely done, although it didn't quite fit her vision. They walked all the way into the alley in the back. There was enough space to park a van for deliveries and enough light for it to feel safe, which Brooke knew Travis would appreciate.

"And here's the kitchen, which I'm sure you'll love. The former owners of the space upgraded all the appliances." Jennifer's heels clicked on the floor as she showed off the huge industrial ovens and sinks. The area had a surprisingly open feeling for a space that wasn't very big overall.

Brooke opened the ovens and looked inside, barely holding in a sigh of joy. They were bigger and better than any ovens she'd ever used before, pristine and modern. The former owners were even throwing in the big, stainless steel prep tables along with the space, which would save her money too. She'd still have to purchase some other smaller appliances that weren't built-in, but Hunter's loan covered more than enough.

"And here's the main area, which you've seen. The space has plenty of outlets in case you'd like to have tables for people to charge their phones or work, and it fits a pretty decent number of people, even with big chairs." Jennifer walked behind the counter. "And there's plenty of space back here, too, and easy access to the back."

Brooke nodded, running her fingers along the countertop. The placement was perfect, but she knew that she would probably replace the material to match everything else. There were already shelves lining the walls that were perfect for decor or glass jars. She imagined them painted the same shade of pink as the shutters outside.

Maybe the chairs could be a nice, contrasting color—maybe a mint green or a simple cream shade. They had to be comfortable, though, the kind you could sink into and not want to leave for hours. She could see them lining the space, with little tables that were just big enough for a laptop, a cup of coffee, and a pastry.

Angela had taken her antique shopping a few months back, and they'd seen some vintage cake stands that were a perfect fit for the aesthetic she wanted to create to display scones and cookies. She had a loose idea of what she wanted for the rest of the details, which she knew Angela would be more than happy to hammer down with her.

Brooke made one more slow turn, taking in the entire space, then smiled.

"I think I want to make an offer," she said, her stomach fluttering. It was nerve-wracking and exciting, all wrapped into one. She could hardly believe that this was happening. Her dreams about the space aligned perfectly with the reality.

"Wonderful!" Jennifer smiled. "We can start on the paperwork back at my office. It's just a short walk a few blocks over if you want to follow me."

Brooke couldn't help but grin the entire walk over to Jennifer's office at Titan Real Estate Partners. Once they got there, the paperwork part was much less exciting, as was all the work on the other permits and things of that sort that she had to do on her own time, but she was willing to do it if it meant getting the bakery space.

Once she finished everything Jennifer needed to start the process on her end, Brooke headed back to Hunter's. Motivated by the rush of getting the space, Brooke grabbed her laptop and settled on the couch with Scratch to work on some of the other forms that she needed to get done. The little black kitten seemed to sense her good mood, because he purred and kneaded her thighs without prompting, as if he was smiling at her too.

Time flew by despite the dryness of the work, and before she knew it, she was ready for a break. She stood up and stretched, rubbing her eyes. Scratch did the same, yawning.

"Do you need a break from all those naps, Scratch?" Brooke asked, laughing and petting his furry head. "Must be hard being a cat. Let's go bake something. Maybe pie crusts for Thanksgiving? It's coming up so fast."

Scratch meowed in response and followed Brooke into the kitchen. She grabbed flour and sugar, then got started on some basic crusts while thinking up a twist on a classic. Travis loved pumpkin pie, and her father loved apple pie, so she would definitely do those. But her mother and Angela were much more adventurous, so she wanted to do something for them too.

Brooke rolled up her sleeves and got to work. Her family was going to love the pies that she came up with, and she couldn't wait to see their faces when they tried them.

CHAPTER TWELVE

"Come in, Hunter!" Andy Paulson, the director of the film Hunter was shooting, grinned broadly as he spoke. "Happy Thanksgiving."

"Happy Thanksgiving to you too," Hunter said.

He smiled and stepped inside Andy's house. Well, *mansion* was probably a better word for it. Andy's home was beautiful both inside and out, and it managed to be luxurious without being gaudy like many of the homes that Hunter had been to in southern California. The entryway was open with a high ceiling and a big, winding staircase down one side. A chandelier made of blown glass hung down from the ceiling, reflecting colored light against the walls.

Andy's wife, Ingrid, had decorated for the

holidays with wreaths and cornucopias, and the scent of warm spices filled the air. Andy led him farther into the house and out onto their back patio, where many of his cast mates were mingling and sipping wine with some of Andy and Ingrid's friends and family. The LA weather was perfect, a far cry from the damp cold he knew that Marigold was experiencing.

They were getting close to wrapping up filming on *Far and Away*, so the entire atmosphere on set had been filled with stress, but now they had the chance to relax together. Andy poured Hunter a glass of wine and checked on everyone else's drinks, stepping around his rescue dog, Izzy, who wanted to be in the middle of the excitement. Hunter gave her a few scratches under the chin before she trotted off to get petted by someone else.

"Hunter, hey!" one of his co-stars, Paolo said, clapping Hunter on the shoulder. "Glad you made it!"

"Hey! It's nice to see everyone fully out of costume for once." Hunter looked out onto the rest of the patio and at the hills in the distance. It was sunset, so everything looked a little golden, steeped in warm colors. "And it's nice to relax a little bit."

"You're telling me." Paolo sipped his wine and

looked over his shoulder at the house. "I'm going to eat so much that the costume department will have to alter my pants."

Hunter laughed and looked where Paolo was looking. The massive dining room table inside was being set up by a catering team, directed by Ingrid. All of the food smelled delicious. It had been a while since Hunter had eaten something anywhere close to a home cooked meal, so he was looking forward to it. He could only live off of take-out for so long and he rarely had the energy to cook after a long day of shooting.

But part of him wished he was back on Marigold, eating a simple homemade Thanksgiving dinner and watching football.

Hunter and Paolo chatted for a few minutes, catching up on the scenes that everyone else was shooting, until Ingrid called everyone in for dinner. The table was heavy with platters of food and decorative centerpieces, and everyone had more than enough space to spread out.

Hunter spotted Saffron across the room, laughing, and she caught his eye. He nodded in her direction and took a seat a little farther away from hers. Having others around made her dial back her flirtatious advances, but not by much. He wanted to relax and enjoy his meal, not think about every single thing he said and wonder if he was giving her the wrong impression about his feelings toward her.

Hunter settled at a corner of the table, and Andy sat down next to him after he made Izzy sit in the corner of the room, out of the way of all the humans. The dog whined a little, but settled, her eyes on her owner. One of her ears quirked up, as if she were listening for a human to give her permission to get a treat.

"Don't mind the pup—she'll give you sad eyes to convince you to drop a piece of meat or a green bean," Andy said. He glanced back at Izzy, whose tail started wagging, and smiled.

"She's pretty convincing with those big eyes. And I don't think I could watch everyone eating all of this without salivating," Hunter said, putting his cloth napkin in his lap. "This is a beautiful spread."

"The credit all goes to Ingrid. She works in event planning, so she knows all the best caterers in town." Andy filled his plate with the sides that were closest to them and then handed the dishes to Hunter. "We like to have a lot of people over for Thanksgiving, and there's no way on earth that we could cook for everyone. Or ourselves."

"Not much of a cook, huh?" Hunter passed a

cloth-lined basket of buttery rolls over to Paolo, who was sitting on his other side talking to Ingrid.

"Nope. I've accidentally lit broccoli on fire, which I didn't know was even possible. I've tried following recipes, and it's still a disaster. I'm just not meant to do more than pop something into the microwave."

"I'm sure you could learn. There are all sorts of resources out there."

"Maybe, with a lot of time and a ton of effort. If I had to separate all of my skills into buckets, normal skills like cooking and organizing would be pretty much empty, but all of my creative ones would be much more full." Andy grinned. "It's a good thing that movies exist. Otherwise I'd be out of luck."

The two of them dug into their food. It was a perfect twist on the traditional Thanksgiving dishes that Hunter was used to, tailored to the guests' various dietary requirements. The stuffing was vegan, but it didn't lack in flavor or moisture in the slightest, and they had gone with duck instead of turkey, which was much juicier.

Some cranberry sauce got passed around, made from real cranberries instead of the canned gelatin stuff that Hunter remembered from childhood. Some dishes had an international flair in honor of the actors and crew who were from other countries. Hunter was grateful that they were all able to come together—everyone deserved to spend the holiday with good company, enjoying a delicious meal.

"I'm really happy with how your scenes are turning out," Andy said after topping off Hunter's wine. "I was just looking at some unedited footage before dinner."

"Because you just can't take a day off," Ingrid said, momentarily pulled from her conversation. She shot her husband an amused glance, which he returned, before she went back to talking to Paolo.

"I can't help myself. It's basically an illness at this point." Andy shrugged and smiled, his boyish expression making him seem younger than forty-two. "But anyway, your performance is stellar. I can't wait to see how it all shapes up. I'd love to have a shoot of this quality again."

"Thank you," Hunter said, a pleased smile spreading across his face. He hoped that Andy was hinting at them working together for a second time. "It's been a dream, honestly."

And it was. Hunter didn't mind doing blockbusters since they were fun in their own way, from seeing how some scene filmed in front of a green screen turned into something entirely different at the end, to the press events at conventions filled with screaming fans. Plus, they paid the bills very handsomely.

But Hunter loved this work, too. He enjoyed working with his co-stars and all the other actors on set, and Andy brought out the best in everyone's acting abilities. Hunter easily imagined his future career unfolding in this direction, with more satisfying and rewarding days on set and more serious roles that he could immerse himself in.

"Fingers crossed that everything in post-production runs smoothly. I doubt we'll run into trouble since the effects aren't too specialized and the marketing team is already doing good work, but some of my projects have gotten off to a rough start despite a perfect shoot." Andy sighed. "That happened to my most recent film, which is finally coming out soon."

"*Stargazer*, right?" Hunter had heard of the film since the buzz around it had been simmering for a long time. It was a romantic drama between an astronaut and his wife, set across several decades.

"Yup. It's finally done." Andy looked relieved. "I'd love to have you and a guest come to the premiere. It should be great—I'm really proud of how it turned out, struggles aside."

"That would be amazing, thank you," Hunter said.

The red carpet madness around premieres usually put Hunter off, but he was more than happy to weather that if it meant seeing a great movie. Half of the reason why Hunter had been interested in a role in *Far and Away* in the first place was because of Andy's work. The up-and-coming director's films were eclectic, but they all had a signature flavor, focusing on stories of real people in unusual situations. Hunter knew that this movie they were working on was going to have the same feel by the time it was over.

Hunter asked Andy about *Stargazer*'s inspiration and all of the ins and outs of what had happened after the shoot had ended. Andy was a great storyteller, and before Hunter knew it, their entire half of the table was hanging on his every word, laughing late into the evening. After some coffee and dessert, Hunter yawned.

"Going to head home and enter a food coma?" Paolo asked, putting his light jacket on. It was hardly cool enough for one, but everyone's cold tolerance in LA was much lower than back in Marigold.

"Yup, probably." Hunter glanced at his phone,

making sure the car he'd called for was on the way. "Have a good night."

"You too."

Hunter's ride came eventually, and he hopped in. Even though most of the food had been delicious, he didn't feel that warm, deep satisfaction that he sometimes had after meals back in Marigold. That was probably because of the dessert he had chosen, which was a chai-spiced pumpkin pie, plus some freshly made ice cream. There were other basic kinds of pie, like apple, but he'd wanted to try something different. He'd gotten a taste of the other options too from cast members who were willing to spare a bite for him. He would have found all of them completely wonderful before he'd tried Brooke's baking. But now, nothing else could compare.

With the sweet blonde baker on his mind, he texted Brooke to see if she was still awake or if she had fallen into a food coma. Her response came back almost immediately, letting him know she was awake. He called her up, deciding he'd rather hear her voice than text.

"Hey, happy Thanksgiving!" Brooke said as she answered.

"Happy Thanksgiving to you too. How was your dinner?"

"Ugh, amazing. The only reason I'm awake is because I had coffee with dessert. I half-wished I could get taken home in a wheelbarrow, I was so stuffed." Brooke chuckled. "Mom and Dad go super traditional with the main meal—stuffing, turkey, green bean casserole, stuff like that. But this year I went crazy with the pies and desserts. We had some extended family over, plus some friends, and everyone ate everything up like vultures."

"I'm jealous." Hunter laughed. "What desserts did you make? Describe them to me, so I can sit here across the country and stew in envy."

"Apple and pumpkin for Travis and my dad, who would be devastated to sit through Thanksgiving dinner without those on the other end. But then I made bourbon pecan pie, pumpkin bread pudding, and pumpkin pie brownies."

"I'm so incredibly jealous that I don't know what to do with myself," Hunter said with a groan. "All of it sounds good, but that bourbon pecan pie sounds like a dream."

"I can make you one when you get back. Mom loved it too, so I'll be making one for them for their freezer," Brooke said. "How was your dinner? It was at your director's house, right?"

"Yup, it was at Andy's. Dinner was great, but the desserts were just okay—pumpkin pie, apple pie, things like that. There are a lot of people who are vegan or gluten-free or dairy-free, so I sampled those desserts, too. They were better than the regular pies, to my surprise."

"Lots of desserts can be delicious without dairy or gluten, like macarons. I make killer macarons, though they can be a total pain to make." He heard Brooke turn on some water and then turn it off in the background. "They're a little fussy, but cute. Like Scratch here, who seems to have lost his mind. I gave him some leftover turkey, and now he won't leave me alone. I'm out of snacks, buddy!"

"Once you give them human food, they'll never stop asking for more." Hunter grinned, thinking of Izzy the dog. "My director Andy has this adorable dog who stared at us all through dinner with the saddest eyes. Someone finally relented and gave her a bit of duck toward the end. She was the happiest pup I've ever seen."

Brooke laughed. "I would be thrilled if I were that dog. I've only had duck once in my life."

"It was great." Hunter hopped out of the car and

thanked his driver when the car pulled to a stop outside his building. "Speaking of Andy, he invited me to a premiere for one of his movies. Would you like to go with me? I wanted to thank you for watching the house."

Brooke paused. "Wait, what? A movie premiere? In Hollywood?"

"Yup."

"But..." She let out a short breath, then laughed. "That's too much! You're already paying me to watch your house, *and* you invested in my business. You don't owe me anything."

"If you put it that way, maybe I don't, but I'm not putting it that way." Hunter shrugged, digging for his keys. "I just want to bring you. The movie is supposed to be phenomenal, too, and you'll get to see it before everyone else."

"I'd love to go!" Brooke made a little sound of happiness, as if she'd tried to hold back a squeal but failed. "This is so cool! I've never been on a red carpet before."

"Great! I'll make arrangements for a hotel room for you while you're here." Hunter opened the door to his condo and flipped on the lights. "Do you want me to get you a dress? I'm more than happy to. Well, I'm more than happy to get someone who knows something about women's fashion to help me get one for you."

"No, no, I've got the dress part down," Brooke said. "I'm so excited!"

She yawned as she finished speaking, despite her cheerful tone, and Hunter smiled.

"Excited but tired?" he asked, throwing his keys into the basket next to the door and kicking off his shoes.

"Yup. I should head to bed before I fall asleep standing up. Talk to you later. Good night!"

"Bye, good night."

He hung up, still smiling, and went to go change into something more comfortable—with a little more give around the waist. Premieres had become a little old hat to him, but the idea of going to one with Brooke made the idea appealing all over again.

CHAPTER THIRTEEN

"I haven't been this excited to go clothes shopping in a while," Brooke said, opening the door to the cute dress boutique that a friend of hers had recommended. It was just off Main Street, not far from all of her favorite places downtown.

"Have you *ever* been that excited to go clothes shopping?" Angela asked, stepping in behind her and holding the door for Lydia.

"Well, sometimes." Brooke lived in comfortable clothes she could move in—leggings, soft shirts, sweatshirts. Baking in a tight blouse and jeans wasn't fun, and neither was paying to dry clean a flour covered shirt. "But how often do I get to shop for a dress to wear on the red carpet?"

The boutique was lined with sparkling dresses,

arranged by color, then by length. A mannequin was wearing a pale green gown with a short train, which Brooke gravitated toward. It looked glamorous without going overboard. Angela and Lydia wandered over to other racks, absently picking through choices.

"Let me know if I can help you with anything," the salesperson said from behind the desk.

Brooke smiled and thanked her, then went to the rack of green dresses near the door. She was happy to be left to her own devices. Sometimes shopping with a salesperson breathing down your neck, urging you to buy something, was stressful.

"So what style are you thinking?" Angela asked, picking up a frilly pink dress. She wrinkled her nose and put it back. "What's big in Hollywood right now?"

"I have no idea. I don't think I'd want to wear anything trendy, though. Just something nice." Brooke ran her fingers over the green dress that was on the mannequin and looked at it more closely. Now that she was touching it, the fabric felt scratchy and uncomfortable. She put it back. "What do you guys think? What color?"

"Blue, maybe?" Lydia held up a dark blue strapless gown. It was snug through the bodice but flared out in a mermaid style around the knees. "It would look so nice with your blonde hair, and the darker blue would complement the blue of your eyes."

"Oh, that's beautiful! I'll try that on," Brooke said. The salesperson took the dress and hung it on the back of the door of a dressing room.

"Or maybe something with a little sparkle and drama if you'll be photographed?" Angela pulled a red dress with a higher neckline lined with sparkly beads that dipped low in the back. It was much more daring than anything Brooke had ever worn before, but she liked it.

"Sure, might as well try it on."

"I can't believe you're going to a big movie premiere," Lydia said, grinning. "We'll need every single detail when you get back, from the carpet itself to the bathrooms."

Brooke laughed. "The bathrooms? Really?"

"Why not? Maybe they do something fancy to them if there are a lot of famous people there. Like lounges to take a breather in and warm towels for your hands." Lydia shrugged, picking up a magenta dress and holding it out in front of herself to get a better look. "Do you think they'll have those gift bags with all the expensive stuff inside? Or is that just at the Oscars?"

"I think that's just at the Oscars." Brooke pulled a black dress from the rack and put it with the other ones on the back of the dressing room door. "I think this is just low key. Well, as low key as a movie premiere can be."

"What celebrities will be there?" Angela asked.

"I have no idea! I bet there will be a lot. The director has done a lot of big movies." Brooke grabbed one more dress on a whim. It was somewhere between cream and blush pink, with swaths of chiffon crisscrossed tightly around the bodice before flowing out softly from the waist down. Something about it called to her.

Once she had plenty of things to try on, the salesperson opened the dressing room for her and she went inside.

"Keep an eye out for anyone famous," Angela said from outside the small dressing room. "Make a list on your phone if you have to. All the A-listers, of course. And the B-listers."

Brooke kicked off her boots, smiling and shaking her head. "So basically every celebrity you've ever seen in 'People' magazine or in an Oscar-nominated movie in the past five years?"

"Pretty much," both Angela and Lydia said immediately.

All three women laughed.

"Okay, I'll definitely keep an eye out, then."

Brooke stepped into one of her first dresses, the dark blue strapless gown that Lydia had picked out. She zipped it as much as she could before stepping out, and Angela helped her zip it up the rest of the way. Brooke looked at herself in the three-way mirror and shrugged. It reminded her of her senior prom dress, though she looked much more sophisticated.

"It's nice," Brooke said. "But I'm not sure. I guess I should try on the others to see how they measure up against each other."

She went back into the dressing room to try on the next one, which was a bit of a hassle to put on. The crisscrossing straps looked lovely on the hanger, but they were a tangled mess off of it. She was going to be getting dressed by herself in the hotel room before the premiere, so this was probably out of the running based on the effort it took to put on alone.

"How's everything going with the bakery?" Angela asked. "How was it after you saw it?"

"It was amazing," Brooke said, adjusting the complicated set of straps on her shoulders. "Even better than I imagined. I put in an offer on the space already."

"Wow, it's really happening!" Lydia said. "That's so exciting."

"And so scary." Brooke finally got the last strap into place and stepped outside.

"Definitely scary." Angela nodded and fluffed out the dress's train when Brooke stepped in front of the mirror. "How do you like this one?"

Brooke examined herself in the mirror. The dress was pretty, but trendy, and the color didn't look quite right with her skin or hair. It felt like it belonged on someone else.

"It's a little bit too edgy for me, I think." She headed back into the dressing room. "But anyway, I've been so worried. I keep checking my email to see if Jennifer has gotten back to me yet about whether the offer was accepted."

"That reminds me of when we were bidding on the inn." Lydia sighed, her tone nostalgic. "It was so unbelievably stressful, but when we got it, it felt so freeing."

"And then it got even more stressful really fast." Angela laughed. "But it's been so worth it."

Brooke understood. The daily rollercoaster of emotions—excitement to stress to defeat to excitement again—was a lot to handle, but her excitement tended to win. Plus, she saw what she could have on the other side in Lydia and Angela. They had taken the plunge and were now doing incredibly rewarding work. The inn was doing fabulously, and they were both happier than ever. Brook was just grateful to be in this little club of women who had leapt into being business owners with both feet.

Once she managed to extract herself from the trendy dress, she grabbed the blush pink chiffon one that was her last pick. It was easy to put on—all she had to do was step inside and put her arms through the sleeves. She could even zip it up by herself. The inside was just as soft and silky as the outside.

"What about this one? It's really cozy." Brooke stepped out of the dressing room, and both Angela and Lydia gasped.

"You look so gorgeous!" her sister said, clasping her hands together.

"So beautiful!" Lydia agreed. "The whole look is very Grace Kelly."

As Brooke looked at herself in the mirror, she had to agree. She was used to seeing herself in casual clothes, but being in this dress felt just as *right* as her usual outfits, both in how it fit with her personality and how it felt on her body. It was incredibly comfortable despite looking so fancy.

"I love it. I think this is the one." Brooke beamed and turned, looking at herself from every angle.

The blush pink color complemented her perfectly, and it fit like it was custom made for her. It wasn't cutting edge or trendy, but she looked classy and sophisticated. It was timeless. She could easily imagine her hair up in a classic chignon, her makeup done tastefully. She was due for a haircut soon anyway, and she hoped that her stylist could show her how to do some kind of simple updo herself. Now all she needed were comfortable shoes to match the dress and complete the ensemble.

She did one more turn before heading back into the dressing room, feeling pretty and elegant. She could hardly wait for Hunter to see her in this.

* * *

Jennifer sat in her office, sipping her third cup of herbal tea of the day. It was warm and spicy, perfect for such a cold day. She loved showing houses, but she was glad that she didn't have to venture out into the drizzle right now.

"I can't believe it!" Her coworker Rita's voice

floated into her office from down the hall. "The back window was smashed in and glass was everywhere. It was such a mess and took forever to clean. It didn't look like stuff was taken, but it was still a little scary.

Jennifer paused, her brow furrowing, then went into the hall. Rita and her other coworker, Bill, were standing near the mini kitchen, nursing cups of coffee. Rita was dressed in the outfit she typically wore when showing houses, so Jennifer assumed she had just gotten back from a showing.

"Rita, did you say there was a break-in at one of the properties you're handling?" Jennifer asked.

"Yeah." The older woman nodded, looking distressed. "Thankfully, the house was empty."

"That happened to one of the houses I was trying to sell a few months back." Jennifer pulled her phone from the pocket of her skirt. "The police officer on the scene gave me the number to his direct line and told me to call if any other break-ins happened. What area was it in?"

"It was on the north-east side of the island, a single-family home in the Ladd's Point neighborhood." Rita sighed, then told her the specific address. "It's such a lovely home, too."

"I'll give him a call and report it." Jennifer put

the address in a note on her phone and went back into her office.

Travis's card had sat inside her desk for months, right next to her Post-It notes where she saw it every day. She pulled it out and called him, nerves twisting in her gut ever so slightly. She wasn't sure why, so she took a sip of her tea to calm her stomach.

"This is Travis Collins," he said when he picked up.

"Hi Travis, this is Jennifer from Titan Real Estate Partners. You gave me your card when you responded to my call about that break-in a few months back?"

"Ah, right," he said, his voice warm. "How are you? Is everything okay?"

"No, unfortunately. One of my coworkers mentioned that a house she was going to show had a break-in similar to the one that I came across, so I just wanted to let you know." Jennifer rubbed his card between her fingers.

"Thank you for letting me know. We've had a few more break-ins like yours in the past few months, so it's definitely a pattern. Someone is targeting vacant houses." His voice turned serious. "Do you have an address?"

Jennifer told him the address and more details about the situation.

"Yup, that fits the pattern exactly," Travis said once she finished.

"That's a little scary." Jennifer fiddled with her starfish necklace. "I wouldn't have thought this would happen in that area of Marigold. Or anywhere on the island, really."

"Do you work with a lot of sellers in that area, or show a lot of houses?" he asked. She could easily imagine the concern in his blue-green eyes, even through the phone.

"Recently, no, but I have a few properties I'm selling there."

"Do you go show them alone, or does an associate come with you?"

"I mostly go alone, though usually prospective buyers come later." She paused. "Should I start going with someone else?"

"To be safe, yes. If you ever feel unsafe at a house, call and we'll help you."

"Thank you."

Even though she didn't have a showing scheduled there for a while, Jennifer felt grateful knowing she would be safe when she did go back. Travis had a way of speaking that made her feel incredibly reassured. He felt competent in general, like the kind of man who you could call for help and who would go above and beyond every time.

"Sorry again about that incident at the restaurant," he said after a pause. "I still feel a little bad about it."

"It was really nothing. Don't worry about it," Jennifer reassured him. "I didn't mean to bump into your girlfriend, and if she was a little crabby, she had the right to be. The wait at Ariana was really long that night, and I can get a little testy when I'm super hungry, too."

"She might have been crabby, but that didn't give her the right to be rude." Travis chuckled. "And she's not my girlfriend—she was just a bad dating app match. It was basically a blind date since we'd only talked for a few days before going out."

"Oof." Jennifer smiled. "Yeah, blind dates can be a little hit or miss."

"They definitely can. She was fine, her rudeness aside, but we just weren't compatible. I'm not sure how much these dating apps actually show who people really are. All the dates I've been on have felt a little like bait and switch experiments."

"Ugh, I know how that can be. Back when I was dating, I tried all of those apps and sites and definitely didn't like it. Too many aggressive guys and too many games. I wondered why I even bothered trying to describe myself accurately for my profile."

She had lasted three whole weeks on dating apps before throwing in the towel. Now she was enjoying her break from dating. If finding someone meant swiping through guys who were either jerks, oblivious to the fact that she was an actual person with wants and needs, or not looking for anything more than a fling, she was happy to stay single.

The sometimes crude or thoughtless messages were bad enough, but the two dates she had gone on were legendary amongst her friends for being terrible. One man took her to an extremely fancy restaurant, made a big show of ordering the most expensive things on the menu—without asking her if that was what she actually wanted—and just happened to "forget" his wallet, leaving Jennifer with the entire bill at the end of the night.

The second date... Jennifer couldn't stop herself from laughing out loud at the thought of it.

"What is it?" Travis asked, sounding amused.

"I was just thinking about this terrible date I went on from an app. It was at a deeply uncomfortable performance art show, where the performers threw eggs at a wall for twenty minutes straight for reasons that I still don't understand," Jennifer said. "Then on top of that, I had to sit through drinks with the man after, where he tried to show off how much he knew about art by droning on and on about the show without letting me get a word in edgewise. Not that I knew what to say, anyway."

"Wow." Travis laughed too. "I've had some bad dates, but I definitely think you've got me beat with that one. That's hall of fame material."

"Yeah. I wear it as a badge of honor," she said with a chuckle.

She didn't know Travis all that well, but she found him very easy to talk to. He had an easy sense of humor, which she liked. And his earnestness made her heart warm. How long had it been since she'd met someone this kind? Most men she knew wouldn't have apologized even once for the bumping incident at the restaurant, but he seemed to genuinely feel bad for his date's rudeness.

"Anyway, we'll start investigating these break-ins more," he told her, his voice turning serious. "In the meantime, consider bringing a buddy with you for showings, or maybe meeting the clients in a public place first and going together."

"Will do. Thanks so much, Travis."

"No problem."

He hung up, and so did Jennifer. She tucked his card back into her desk, making sure it was in a safe spot. She hoped there wouldn't be any more break-ins, but it wouldn't hurt to have his information close. Just in case.

CHAPTER FOURTEEN

"And even if we are not related by blood, I will ensure your son's protection, and yours as well," Hunter said, deeply in character. He gripped Saffron's gloved hand. "Do you understand? You will never have to worry about not having a home."

"I understand. You're a kind man." She squeezed his hand, a tear falling down her cheek and onto her black mourning dress. "And it's what my husband would have wanted, no?"

Hunter sighed, then swallowed. "It is indeed what he would have wanted."

He dropped Saffron's hand and offered his arm to lead her out of the room. Even though Saffron's character was crying, she managed to give him a sinister look from beneath her eyelashes as they broke apart outside the doorway. The glance only lasted for a fraction of a second, but it would give the audience a hint that not all was as it seemed with her character.

As much as his friendship with the actress was sometimes strained by her advances, he loved working with her because of little moments like this one. She was a great actress.

Once she was gone, Hunter walked back to his desk, still in character. He rested his hands on the dark wooden surface and stared down at it as if the world sat on his shoulders. This was one of his character William's biggest scenes, when he realized what a life caring for his brother's widow and son would truly mean for him. He was torn between duty and the widow's conniving ways, which he believed had led to his brother's death. But his sense of duty would win out in the end, as it had throughout the story.

William was unlike any character Hunter had played before—he was complicated and torn in a million different directions, which Hunter hoped he had captured as well as he wanted to. He was going to miss William the way he would miss a friend, something he felt after every shoot wrapped up.

But this felt deeper and more significant. This

was his very last scene on his very last day of the best film he had been a part of, something that his experience in blockbusters couldn't come close to. He let the last moments of being William wash over him as he looked up.

"And, cut!" Andy said. "That was perfect! And I think that's a wrap!"

Hunter broke character and grinned. Andy walked up to him and shook his hand, an equally broad smile on his face.

"I can't believe we're finally here. It feels like we just started yesterday in some ways," Hunter said, unbuttoning his waist-coat to get more comfortable. He never had to wear it again. A few days ago, that would have made him over-the-moon happy, but now he was a little sad about it.

"I know." Andy looked around the set, which was bustling with activity now that the shot was over. "It was great."

"It really was."

"Congrats, Hunter!" Paolo said. He was dressed in street clothes already, but he had stuck around to see the final scenes.

"Thanks, man. It's been so great working with you." He shook Paolo's hand, but Paolo pulled him in for a hug.

"Maybe we'll be lucky enough to do it again." Paolo patted his shoulder and moved on to hug the next person.

Hunter hoped so. Paolo, and many of the others, had become his close friends. They were supportive, funny, and hard-working actors, just as dedicated to their craft as he was. Hunter knew he had grown as an actor in ways he hadn't even realized he could.

Hunter congratulated his other co-stars and the team, his smile broad despite the bittersweet feeling in his heart. He was incredibly proud of what he had done and thrilled with how great the experience had been overall, which made its ending even harder to deal with. He would miss everything about this movie—even the uncomfortable costumes.

But he had something to look forward to, at least. The premiere of *Stargazer* was tonight, and Brooke was probably on a plane somewhere over the Midwest right now. He was excited to see her. As much as he had enjoyed being back in LA while filming, he was even happier knowing he could share the city with Brooke for a little while.

* * *

Brooke had never been to Los Angeles before, so she wasn't sure what to expect. Everything she knew about it was from what friends had told her and what she had seen on TV, so she couldn't wait to fill in the gaps for herself. All she knew was that she was excited to get off the plane to stretch her legs and that someone was supposed to be waiting for her to take her to the hotel. Once she picked up her suitcase from baggage claim, she headed outside and easily found an older man holding a sign that said "Brooke Collins."

"Hi, you must be Brooke. Welcome to Los Angeles," the man said, smiling. He had a gentle energy about him that put Brooke immediately at ease. She hadn't even realized how nervous she was until that moment. "Are you ready to head to your hotel?"

"Thank you! And yes, I'm more than ready."

The man took Brooke's suitcase and put it into the trunk of the town car. The inside was fancier than she'd anticipated, with cozy leather seats and a little box filled with bottled water and snacks. Brooke stared out the window on the ride to the hotel, taking in everything she could. It was so drastically different from Marigold, but in a fun way. She did a little people watching in traffic and looked out at the sprawling cityscape and the palm trees that lined the roads. She couldn't wait to see more.

The hotel was grand on the outside, but even more so on the inside. There was white marble everywhere, and all of the fabrics were lush and expensive-looking. It looked like a palace. All of the staff were incredibly professional, and before she knew it, she had the key to her room. Her mouth dropped open when she took it in.

Even though it was just for her, it was massive, probably as big as her apartment. The decor was just as fancy as the lobby, with a massive king-sized bed with soft sheets and pillows, a heavy mahogany desk, and a dresser, which was below a huge flatscreen TV mounted on the wall. The floor to ceiling windows that made up one wall had a stunning view of the hills and all the buildings tucked into them, the blue sky bright above.

Brooke kicked her shoes off and flopped on the bed, sinking into it. She already felt like a princess, and she hadn't even put on her dress yet. It dawned on her that Hunter could have lived like this all the time if he wanted to. But then again, the fact that he chose to live on Marigold in a nice, but relatively modest home made her like him even more.

She texted Hunter to let him know that she was

in the hotel, then hopped up to get ready. She opened her suitcase, where she had carefully tucked her dress away in a garment bag, and hung it up. She loved it more and more every time she looked at it. By the time she had unpacked her shoes and jewelry, Hunter had texted back telling her he would come pick her up at seven for the premiere.

Brooke took a long shower, cleaning away the travel grime, and slipped on one of the big, fluffy robes that the hotel provided to finish getting ready. Her hair dresser had shown her how to do a simple updo after giving her hair a trim and some new highlights, so Brooke tackled that first. With some wrangling, she was able to replicate what her hair dresser had taught her almost perfectly. It was a low bun, almost like a ballerina's chignon, but with a more intricate twist.

Next came her makeup. She had scoured every blog she could find about red carpet makeup and found a few good tips. Her makeup wasn't as fancy or expensive as the brands the sites had suggested, but she had enough to work with. She watched a little TV as she applied it, not going too heavy with anything. She had borrowed a red lipstick from Angela, and it looked great. She still had a little time, so she put on her dress and then called her sister.

"Hey!" Angela said. "You made it over to the west coast okay?"

"Yup! I'm all settled in at the hotel."

"Have you seen any celebrities yet?"

Brooke laughed. "I've only been in the airport and the hotel, so no. But I know to keep a look out. I even did a little people-watching on the ride over, but none of the people in convertibles were famous."

"Good. And take pictures." Angela laughed too. "How was the flight? And how's the hotel?"

"The flight was fine, but long. And the hotel is absolutely gorgeous. It's the nicest place I've ever been." Brooke ran her hands over the smooth, soft sheets. "I think it's literally the size of my apartment. Stepping into the bathroom is like going to a spa."

"That's so sweet of Hunter to book that for you," Angela said. "When's the premiere?"

"Soon! He's picking me up at seven." Brooke checked the time. "I'm already dressed and made-up. Now I'm just buzzing with nerves since I don't know what it'll really be like surrounded by famous people. But I'm mostly excited."

"Ooh, send a selfie. I want to see your whole look all together."

Brooke laughed and hopped up to take a selfie in

the full-length mirror, then sent it via text. "Okay, it's coming."

Angela paused for a second, then gasped. "Oh, wow! You look so beautiful! You'll fit right in."

"You think?"

"I know."

"Thanks, Angie." Brooke's heart warmed. She was so glad she had called Angela—her older sister always knew how to make her feel good.

"No problem. I've got to go, though. Have fun, okay? And don't forget my celebrity list!"

"I won't. Talk to you later."

Brooke hung up, looking at herself in the mirror again. She touched up her lipstick a little bit, and a few minutes later there was a knock on the door. When she opened it, her breath hitched and her heart fluttered. Hunter was standing there in a tuxedo, his dark hair perfectly styled and pushed out of his face. The dark fabric of the tux made his gray eyes seem both paler and more intense at the same time. He looked even more handsome than usual.

She had gotten used to him in regular clothes over the course of their friendship, so she hadn't seen him in full movie star mode. He seemed larger than life, like someone she should have been looking at through a TV screen and not through a doorway. He was almost intimidating.

But then he smiled. It wasn't his movie star smile —it was his sweet, boyish one that came out when he talked about acting or her baking. His cheeks flushed pink.

"Hey, you look beautiful," he said, almost shyly.

"Thanks." Brooke blushed too. "You look handsome."

They looked at each other for a beat, smiling, before Hunter led her downstairs to the waiting car. The driver whisked them away to the theater.

CHAPTER FIFTEEN

"Ready?" Hunter asked, resting his hand on the car door's handle as he glanced over at Brooke, still stunned by how gorgeous she looked. They had gotten to the theater with minimal traffic, so they were slightly early. "There's going to be a lot of cameras going off, so be ready."

"Gotcha." Brooke nodded and swallowed, clutching her bag. "I'm ready."

He opened the door and got out, then helped Brooke out of the car so that her dress wouldn't catch on the door. Sure enough, the photographers started taking photo after photo of them immediately, shouting his name. Brooke looked momentarily stunned, but he guided her toward the official red carpet with a hand on her back.

He glanced around, noting that several photographers and other guests were looking at him curiously. In a world where who was with whom, and where new relationships made headlines, having Brooke as his guest was probably raising some questions. She was a complete unknown to them.

But none of that mattered to him, not now or even in the recent past. He was proud to have her with him, and she looked even more beautiful than any other woman there. Her dress had an old Hollywood feel and suited her well, the color highlighting her lovely blue eyes. Like he did when he was in Marigold, she usually wore casual clothes. Seeing her dressed up reminded him of just how stunning she was.

They came to a stop, waiting for a handler to let them step onto the carpet. Brooke's eyebrow went up in a silent question as she glanced at him.

"That's something they don't tell you in the magazines—there's usually a little line so that the red carpet won't be too crowded," he explained.

"I can see why they wouldn't mention that. Lines aren't all that glamourous." Brooke laughed, leaning over to see how much longer they had to wait. "But this gives me a little time to calm down. Is my face super red? It feels red. It would be just my luck to look like the carpet itself."

"No, you look perfect," Hunter assured her.

It wasn't long before the handler gestured for them to go. Brooke clutched his arm tightly at first, but soon, she fell into the easy rhythm of stopping for some photos, walking a little farther, then stopping again. By the time they reached the end of the photographer's line and stepped inside the theater where the film was going to be shown, Brooke was grinning, her grip on his arm loose again.

"See, you were a total natural," Hunter murmured.

"Was I?" She laughed. "I think I got hypnotized by all the flashbulbs."

"I can relate to that. No matter how many times I've done this, I'm still surprised by how many photographers there are."

Brooke nodded and looked around the lobby of the theater. It was a beautiful building, a historical movie theater that had been renovated to add more space without losing its vintage charm. It was outfitted to show old films and new ones, especially specialty films with limited runs. Brooke seemed to be in awe of it all, and of all the other people. Her gaze darted from place to place as a small but excited smile played across her lips.

Hunter watched her take it all in, which made him see it with new eyes. He had been to premieres at this theater before, and others, but all of it was so new to her. Her eyes lit up when a waiter handed them flutes of champagne and guided them deeper into the building, and when she saw actors or people she recognized, she squeezed his arm a little and tried to play it cool.

"Angela wanted me to keep an eye out for certain celebrities, and a lot of them are here," Brooke said quietly, looking past Hunter's shoulder for a second. "She gave me a literal list of specific people to look for, like a weird scavenger hunt."

"Who's on it?" he asked.

Brooke dug through her small purse and pulled out her phone, giggling as she showed him the list. He grinned.

"I know a few of them. Maybe we could get some pictures after."

"Really?" Brooke put her phone back in her bag, looking up at him with a huge smile. "That would be amazing! Would it be dorky to ask for an autograph?"

"Not dorky in the slightest," he promised her with a grin.

In fact, Hunter found it refreshing. It was easy to get jaded after living in Hollywood for as long as he had. Events started to blur together, parties became boring, and going out night after night to network got tiring. But there was this amazing side of it too—the experience of seeing something new and getting immersed in a story, the very thing that drew most actors to acting in the first place. Nothing beat going to the movie theater and seeing something on the big screen.

They mingled in the lobby a little bit before heading inside the theater. Most people were hanging out in the broad aisles since the movie wasn't starting for another ten minutes.

"Excuse me for a second. I should probably go to the bathroom before it starts so I won't have to miss any of it," Brooke said.

"No worries, I'll wait for you."

She headed back outside, leaving Hunter standing next to their row.

As more people trickled into the theater, several more people that he knew came in. He said hello and made a little small talk, promising to talk more after the film screening was over. There were going to be some refreshments and more champagne afterward.

"Hunter! Hi!" Saffron called, waving as she entered the theater. "Andy invited you too?"

"Hey! Yeah, he did," Hunter said. Her long yellow dress swished around her legs as she made her way toward him.

"I didn't get the chance to say congrats again after we wrapped earlier today. I had to slip out to start getting ready for this. Otherwise we could have gone out for a drink or something." Saffron sighed a little and looked him over, the interest clear in her eyes. "You were fantastic in that last scene."

"So were you." Hunter smiled politely.

"I hope we get to do it again soon." She smoothed her hand over his lapel as if she were cleaning off a piece of lint and looked up at him through her lashes, smiling. "You look amazing, by the way."

"Thanks. So do you."

And she did look beautiful. Undoubtedly, she'd end up on some best dressed list somewhere. But it was easy to see that she wasn't just talking about his tux, which he'd worn to a different event before. A few people were passing behind Hunter, so he couldn't step away from her right away. He tucked his hands into his pockets and didn't say anything more. He didn't want to give her the wrong idea.

When he could, he took a step back from her,

just as he caught sight of Brooke re-entering the
theater.

* * *

Brooke spotted Hunter next to a beautiful woman
wearing a long yellow dress. They were fairly close
together too, closer than they had to be to make room
for the people milling around them.

She heard the woman say something and laugh,
and a sudden realization clicked in her mind. This
was the woman Brooke had heard in the background
from time to time when she'd talked to Hunter on
the phone. She recognized her voice and her laugh.
The beautiful woman's tone was a musical alto,
which seemed to carry over the sound of the crowd.

Hunter stepped back from the woman and
nodded at something she said before she left, heading
farther down the aisle. As the willowy woman walked
away, Brooke realized it was Saffron, one of Hunter's
co-stars whom he had mentioned off-handedly. She
was a somewhat well-known actor, although not quite
as famous as Hunter Reed. Brooke knew her from a
movie whose title she couldn't recall.

"Hey, ready to head to our seats?" Hunter asked

as Brooke stepped up beside him. She managed to smile and say yes.

He led them to their seats at the other end of the aisle they were on, which had a great view of the screen. She was excited to watch to film, but her happy mood was dampened a little bit by what she had seen. That actress was clearly interested in Hunter, and he didn't seem entirely disinterested in her.

And for some reason, the thought of that stung.

Brooke had tried to get out of the habit of comparing herself to others, but it was hard to resist the urge when she was around the most beautiful people in the world. She suddenly felt like her dress wasn't flattering or fancy enough, and she felt a little foolish for having allowed herself to develop a crush on Hunter.

She settled in her seat as the movie started, trying to focus. But it was impossible. Even as the first images played across the screen, her mind kept running in circles.

Hunter had explicitly told her he was bringing her as a thank you and never promised that it was anything more than just a friendly outing. And honestly, it shouldn't matter whether Hunter was interested in Saffron or not—Brooke wasn't dating Hunter, so he didn't owe her an explanation.

The movie was good, with a blend of beautiful shots on Earth and some set in space, alternating between the astronaut's point of view and his wife's. The score was beautiful, setting the dramatic mood without getting sappy. Still, Brooke couldn't fully let herself go and become immersed in it. Her shoulders were tense, and she kept chewing on her lower lip.

She noticed Hunter glancing at her out of the corner of her eye from time to time, a slightly worried look on his face.

"You okay?" he whispered in her ear after a while.

She wasn't sure how to respond, so she just nodded. Hunter studied her for a bit longer, clearly skeptical even in the dark. Then he shook his head and gently took her elbow, tugging her out of the seat before leading her up the aisle and out into the lobby.

"Are you sure everything is okay? Did something happen? Are you feeling sick?" he asked once they were out. The lobby was mostly empty aside from a few other premiere guests taking a break and some staff members cleaning up.

Concern was written all over Hunter's face, and even a little fear. Shoot. She must really look like a mess. She hadn't realized her thoughts were that clearly visible on her face.

Brooke sighed, her cheeks heating up. Hunter was her friend, and he would never purposefully embarrass her or make her feel stupid. She trusted him enough to tell him the truth—and she didn't want to worry him.

"It's just..." She crossed her arms over her chest as if she were protecting herself. "I just saw what happened between you and Saffron. The flirting. And it's totally fine, but... it just threw me off a bit, I guess. I have... feelings for you, so it stung a little to see that. But if you're seeing her, it's totally fine. She seems great. And I always want to be your friend."

Hunter blinked a few times. Then he grinned, the same cute, boyish one he had given her at the hotel. Stepping a little closer, he gently gripped her elbows.

"It's not like that at all with Saffron. I've been trying to dodge her advances this whole shoot." He squeezed her arms softly. "And I've been dodging her advances because I have feelings for you too."

Brooke's eyes went wide. She blinked a few times, her jaw dropping open as her heart rate skyrocketed. "Wait, really?"

"Yes, really."

She let his words sink in for a few moments before grinning too. Hunter chuckled, pulling Brooke in closer as amusement and warmth shone in his gray eyes. She could hardly believe it. He felt the same way about her as she felt about him? If his hands weren't warm and a little rough on her skin, she would have thought she was dreaming.

Hunter tilted her head up with one hand, and her breath caught in her throat as their gazes locked. He brushed his thumb over her cheek, making a little shiver run down her spine, and then dropped his head to press his lips softly to hers. Brooke's heart nearly beat out of her chest, and it took all of her willpower to not grin even wider against his mouth.

"Ready to head back inside, then?" Hunter asked as they broke apart, threading his fingers through hers.

"Yeah, definitely."

She let him lead her back into the darkened theater, the wide, giddy smile still on her face. The movie was still playing, but she was sure she wouldn't be able to pay attention to it at all. Now she was distracted in a whole different way than she had been earlier, and for a much better reason.

CHAPTER SIXTEEN

"Did you enjoy your stay?" Angela asked the guest checking out of the inn.

"I loved it. It was so nice to have a place to stay that wasn't with family," the man said with a smile. "As much as I love them, I love having privacy more."

"I bet." Angela chuckled as she started closing out his reservation on the computer. She saw the front door open and a familiar blonde head come through.

"And it's so close to the beach, so I loved being able to get that fresh air through my window every day." The man sighed. "I'll definitely stay here again when I visit. I have family all over this area."

"I'm glad to hear it! We're happy to have you any time."

Angela printed off his receipt and handed it to him to sign. He thanked her, and she smiled.

"You're so welcome. Take care, and have a safe trip home!"

The man grabbed his bags and left, bringing Brooke into Angela's view. Her younger sister was beaming, and she even looked a little tanner than she had when she'd left Marigold the other day.

"You're back!" Angela hopped up and hugged her. "How are you? How was the trip?"

"I'm so good!" Brooke said. "And it was absolutely amazing. Everything from the hotel to the movie to the theater. And I have some selfies with celebs from your list for you to look at and even a few autographs."

"Really?" Angela brightened.

"Oh yeah. I saw nearly everyone on your list. Hunter knew a lot of them," Brooke waved her hand, as if she saw celebrities all the time now. "But more importantly, I confessed my feelings for Hunter, and he feels the same way!"

Angela's eyes widened. "Oh my god, wow! That's amazing!"

"I know! It was so great." Brooke's gaze turned

dreamy. "After the movie—which you definitely have to see once it's released everywhere because it's *so* amazing—we just walked and talked for a while, holding hands. It was so lovely just getting to hang out with him and relax since we've mostly been talking on the phone for the past few months. I'm so glad I went with comfortable shoes, or I would be in a world of hurt right now."

Angela smiled, happy to see her sister happy. Still, she couldn't help but worry a tiny bit. Hunter was a nice man, but now they were tied through business and romance. One of either kind of relationship could be a lot, but both at the same time could complicate things.

But she didn't want to spoil Brooke's happiness when it was so fresh, so she just squeezed her sister's arms.

"I'm so happy for you two," she said.

"Thank you. I should try to get back into the swing of things—I just wanted to stop in to say hi. Hunter's on his way back from LA, so I have to swing by his house later, and I have a lot of things to do for the bakery." Brooke stretched. "My vacation is definitely over. I'll be in the kitchen checking in on things if you need me."

The sunny blonde woman headed back toward

the kitchen after giving Angela another hug, leaving her at the front desk alone again. The rest of the morning passed by quickly until Patrick arrived to pick her up for lunch. They had gotten in the habit of going out once or twice a week, sometimes more often if Patrick's writer's block was acting up.

They went to a small bistro that was a short drive from the inn and settled into a small booth. It was chilly out, so both of them opted for some hearty black bean chili and freshly baked bread. It was the perfect lunch, and she couldn't wait to eat it.

While Brooke had been in LA, Kathy had covered for her. Before she'd left Marigold, Brooke had prepared a bunch of batters and doughs that Kathy had just needed to pop into the oven. They were good, of course, but not as good as when Brooke made them fresh the night before. Angela had only eaten part of a muffin that morning because of it.

"Is something on your mind?" Patrick asked once the waiter had taken their orders, his green eyes soft with concern. "You seem a little down or distracted or something."

"I'm just thinking about my sister. She went to a movie premiere with Hunter Reed, and it turns out that they both have feelings for each other. So now Hunter is both her business partner and her boyfriend." Angela sighed. "I'm a little worried for her. Hunter's famous, first of all, even if he lives here, so that adds another unknown element to all of this. And mixing business and romance can go very wrong, very fast."

Patrick nodded, taking in her words thoughtfully, as he always did.

"I can see why that's concerning." He took a piece of bread from the small basket the waiter had brought and buttered it. "But from what I've seen, Brooke and Hunter are very compatible. It doesn't seem like it will be just a fling. Plus, from what I know of him, he's a pretty level-headed guy. If something happens and they break up or the relationship doesn't work out, I doubt he would take it out on Brooke. But there's no reason to think that things will go south."

Angela mulled that over, thinking of the two of them together. They did seem to get along quite well, and Hunter was very kind. The fact that he was still friendly and relatable, even after years of being famous, made Angela like him even more.

"That's true." She grabbed some bread too, the weight coming off her shoulders as she picked up the knife to butter her slice.

"After all, when it's meant to be, it's meant to be." Patrick grinned knowingly as he spoke.

Angela grinned too, completely understanding what he meant. "You're definitely right about that."

* * *

The next evening, Brooke stretched her legs out on her small couch and balanced her laptop on her lap. Hunter had just returned from LA, and now that she was back to living in her apartment instead of house-sitting for him, she had to get used to the small space again. Scratch seemed to be adjusting too. He wedged himself between Brooke's thigh and the back of the couch, purring.

"You just love being in the way, don't you?" she muttered with a snort, petting Scratch's belly. "Or is it because my computer is warm? Are you using it as your personal space heater?"

Scratch just yawned in response. Brooke adjusted her laptop a little so that Scratch wouldn't accidentally turn it off with his paw and opened up some paperwork for the bakery that she had been putting off. It was all administrative stuff—she was quickly learning that the admin work was never-ending when you owned a small business—so she decided to put on a movie to help pass the time.

She snorted quietly to herself as she selected an adventure movie that Hunter had starred in several years ago. He had told her about filming it on their walk after the premiere, and how hilarious and occasionally terrifying it had been to do a lot of his own stunts for the first time. He'd managed to make it look easy on screen even though he had struggled sometimes during the shoot.

She smiled to herself, thinking about the night of the premiere. If she hadn't been jet-lagged, and if Hunter hadn't been worn out from a day of filming, she knew they would have stayed out even later, just walking and talking. It had been perfect. She could hardly believe that it had taken her so long to realize that she had feelings for him. The feelings had grown so slowly and only snapped into focus when she saw him with Saffron.

And he liked her too, which was the best part of it all.

She watched Hunter's character go sliding down a sand dune, which he had told her about. It had given him a massive friction burn. She half-watched the movie and half-worked, which was easy to do because the plot wasn't very complicated. It was a big summer blockbuster, complete with explosions and car chase scenes.

Hunter smiled on screen during a break in the action, and Brooke bit her lip to stop herself from grinning too hard. She knew the real Hunter's smile, and it was even more amazing in real life. She adored the way a dimple appeared in his cheek when he grinned, and how his eyes brightened when he looked at her. The real Hunter was so much better than anything she'd ever dreamed of. Definitely better than any fantasy that existed on screen.

Her phone rang a few moments later, and she paused the movie, glancing down at the small screen. It was Travis.

"Hey, what's up?" she said after she swiped to answer.

"Just wanted to say hey. You're back in Marigold, right?" Travis asked. He sounded a little tired, but upbeat.

"Yup, I am." Brooke stretched a little. She had been hunched over her laptop a little too long.

"How was it rubbing shoulders with the rich and famous?"

"It was amazing." She grinned. "I can see how going to movie premieres and stuff all the time would be exhausting, but going to one for just one night was incredible. The movie was incredible too. We all have to go see it when it comes out in its full theatrical release. Oh, and Hunter and I are seeing each other now."

"Wow, that's great news." Travis chuckled. "So you went to LA and brought a famous movie star boyfriend home as a souvenir?"

Brooke snorted and would have playfully smacked him if they were talking in person. "If you have to boil it way, way down, you might be five percent right. What about you? How are the dating apps? Didn't you go on another date last week?"

"Yeah, I did." Her brother let out a heavy sigh. "It was pretty awkward. Even though her profile seemed nice, we just didn't click. I was sure we would, though, just based on what she wrote. But now I'm wondering if anyone tells the truth on those dating site bios. Or maybe it's just hard to really capture your full personality in just a few lines of text."

"I'm sorry." Brooke hated that Travis was struggling with dating. He was a great person, caring and easy-going. Any woman would be lucky to have him. "What happened?"

"Thanks," he said. "We went to dinner and had nothing to talk about. On the app date I went on before that, a similar thing happened, but she at least tried to talk. This time, we sat there in silence for half the meal. At least she wasn't rude—that other date I just mentioned was pretty rude to someone she accidentally bumped into."

"Oof, that stinks."

"Yeah. I've deleted all the apps off my phone. Even if it takes longer, I just want to let things happen naturally. So if I meet someone, I meet someone. If I don't... well, I don't."

"I'm sure you'll meet someone," Brooke said, completely confident in her words.

"I hope. It feels like all the good ones are taken already."

He sighed again. It sounded like he was speaking from experience, but Brooke knew that Travis wouldn't let out all his secrets to her when he was in a vulnerable place. She just hoped that whoever had caught his eye would notice him soon.

CHAPTER SEVENTEEN

Hunter stretched and rolled over, taking in the scent of his detergent on his pillows. It was great to be home. As much as he enjoyed the place that he had been staying in LA, nothing beat waking up in Marigold. His bedroom had a great view of the ocean most of the time, but today it was a little foggy, making it look like the water was blending into the sky.

He rolled out of bed and got dressed before heading into his kitchen. It was already ten in the morning, much later than he had gotten up in a while. But he didn't have anywhere to be until later, so he was happy to take a lazy day. After months of getting up early to be on set on time, he felt like he deserved it.

He dug through his fridge, where his groceries were lined up neatly thanks to Brooke. She had accepted the delivery and made sure that everything was perfect for when he got home. There was even a container of her cinnamon scones on the counter with a note on how to best reheat them, signed with a heart.

Hunter grinned and turned on the oven to preheat before starting to make some espresso. Brooke's thoughtfulness was one of his favorite things about her.

As he pulled an espresso shot, his phone rang. It was Mimi, his agent.

"Hey, good morning," he said, balancing his phone between his shoulder and ear as he frothed up a little milk. "It's the crack of dawn over there. What's going on?"

"Oh, you know how I am. I need to get through at least an hour's worth of emails before I even finish my coffee." The energetic woman laughed. "I wanted to call you because many of those emails are about you. I swear, I get emails about roles for you every single day at this point."

"You do?" Hunter poured the milk over his espresso shot.

"Definitely, hun. You're heating up. I have more

potential jobs for you than ever," Mimi told him excitedly. "Dramas, mostly, although there's a mix of potential blockbusters in there. Are you interested?"

"Nah, not right now." Hunter grinned, putting his scone into the oven to warm up. "I need time off. I moved all the way out here to Marigold to get a break, and I want to enjoy it."

Brooke was a big part of that decision, too. He wanted to see how things would play out between the two of them, and as much as they enjoyed talking over the phone, it wasn't the same as being in a relationship in person. He missed little moments of affection and the feeling of seeing someone face to face instead of through a screen.

It had been a while since he had liked a woman as much as he liked Brooke. Just being around her lifted his spirits and made him see life differently. He wanted to have every moment he could with her.

Plus, he wanted to see her bakery open and be there for her during that process, especially the taste testing. Things were coming along quickly.

"All right," Mimi said with a sigh. "Some of these offers are going fast."

"I know. But I trust that other things will come along," Hunter said. "Especially since I have the best agent in the world."

"You're too much, you sweet talker." The older woman snorted, and he chuckled. "I've got to get going. Talk soon, okay?"

"Okay, bye."

Hunter hung up and pulled his scone from the oven a few moments early. It wasn't as hot as a freshly baked one, but he couldn't wait. It was still delicious as always—just crumbly enough, with little bursts of cinnamon here and there. He took his time eating breakfast and drinking his coffee, listening to some podcasts he hadn't gotten around to yet.

Once he was done, he puttered around the house. The cleaning service had come before he returned, and Brooke had handled his grocery delivery, so he didn't have much to tidy up. Instead, he unpacked his bags, did a little decluttering, and started making chili for the next day. Before he knew it, it was time for him to get dressed to go pick Brooke up for their first official date.

He drove over to her apartment and knocked on the door.

"Coming!" Brooke called from inside. He heard some shuffling on the inside and soon she opened the door. "Hey!"

"Hey!" Hunter leaned in and kissed her on the cheek, then studied her. She was wearing a simple outfit—a magenta sweater, jeans, and boots, with a touch of makeup—but she looked just as pretty as she had the night of the premiere. "You look great."

"Thanks! So do you." She took his hand and squeezed it before stepping out of her apartment. "Ready to eat?"

"More than ready." Hunter watched her lock her door. "All I've had to eat today is one of the scones you left me. Thank you for those."

"It's no problem, really. I doubted that you'd want to cook on your first morning back." Brooke took his hand again and Hunter led them to his car.

They caught up a little as Hunter drove them to a seafood restaurant, The Fish House, that they had both heard great things about. It was a cozy, intimate space, and the inside was the perfect protection from the wintery chill outside. Everything was freshly caught, and several crab dishes were on special. They decided to go with crab cakes and crab risotto, along with a bottle of white wine.

"As much as I dislike it getting chillier, it's worth it for all the warm foods," Hunter said. "Hearty meals just taste better when there's a bit of a bite in the air."

"I bet it's a harsh change from LA." Brooke smiled. "The winters here can be pretty brutal.

We're lucky we haven't gotten much snow yet, but it's still a lot colder than Southern California."

"Yeah, it's been a bit of a rough adjustment. I'm glad I have a fireplace and a great heating system. I've lost my cold tolerance over the years being in California." Hunter chuckled.

"I bet. You grew up with New England winters though, right?" Brooke asked.

They had chatted about their childhoods a little bit over the phone, so Brooke knew the basics—he'd grown up in a little town a lot like Marigold and had left when he was eighteen to try to break into the acting business.

"I did. And I hated the cold winters back then, too. This time of year is okay, since it's not that brutal, bone-deep cold yet." Hunter waited as the waiter returned, pouring their wine. He thanked the man, who nodded politely before heading off to see to another table. "And sometimes the changes of season are nice. There were times when months would pass by in California, and I'd barely realize that it was getting close to the holidays because the climate is pretty steady."

"Wow, that's weird to think about." Brooke fiddled with one of her small pearl earrings. "The seasons here are everything to me. Spring produce. Summer festivals. The leaves changing in the fall."

"Yeah." He studied her face and smiled at the dreamy look he found there. He and Brooke had gotten to know each other well over their phone calls, but there was so much he didn't know yet. He couldn't wait to know more about her.

"I wish I'd had the chance to explore LA more, although our walk was great," Brooke said. "I can see why people are drawn there. It has a cool vibe."

"Yeah. Maybe we can visit again sometime," he said. "It's even more beautiful once you get out of the city a bit. There's a bit of everything in California, from deserts to mountains to forests. And generally, the people are friendly."

"Are they friendly in Hollywood? Everyone we spoke to at the premiere was so nice."

"Depends on the circles you run in. There are good people and there are bad people, just like there are in any town. Many of the people I met in my last shoot were some of the best people I've ever known," Hunter said. "And it depends on what you're looking for. If you're just looking for friendship, it can be hard to find because people are always trying to get their next role. But I've had good luck. Dating, though. That's a lot harder."

"Yeah?" Brooke sipped her wine, her eyes bright with curiosity.

"Yeah. I haven't dated a lot, actually," he admitted. "Especially when I was in all those blockbusters. It was hard to find people who were genuinely interested in me for who I was instead of what I could do for them."

Brooke's eyes softened. "That sounds so tough. It's impossible to start a relationship if you don't trust someone's motives."

Hunter glanced past Brooke's shoulder for a moment, trying to relax. He rarely opened up like this to anyone, but he had been talking with Brooke for so long that he knew he could be honest with her.

"It's always been a little hard for me to get close to people and trust them in general. I never had a close relationship with my mom, and my dad died when I was five. And then when my career started blowing up, the rest of the family that hadn't spoken to me in ages suddenly appeared like we were old pals."

"Ugh, how awful."

"Yeah. But I cut them out of my life and built a new family with some of my good friends. People I can trust." He smiled a little. "And I trust you, for the record."

She grinned. "I trust you, too."

Hunter reached across the table and took her hand, giving it a little squeeze. It had been a long time since he'd told anyone that, and it had never been more true than it was in that moment.

* * *

Brooke loved the feel of Hunter's large, warm hand wrapped around hers. They didn't let go of each other's hands until the crab cakes came, sharing a brief moment as they grinned at each other. The waiter probably thought they looked like two moony-eyed teenagers, but she didn't care.

Once the waiter left, they dug into the food. The crab cakes were perfect—creamy and flavorful on the inside, with a delicate crust on the outside. Having grown up in Massachusetts, Brooke had had a lot of crab cakes in her life, and these were among the best.

The conversation flowed easily throughout dinner, drifting from humorous topics like Scratch's latest antics to more serious ones, like where Hunter saw his career going. Soon, they were ready for dessert and decided on carrot cake and a chocolate tart to split.

Hunter let Brooke take the first bite of the carrot

cake as he took a bite of the chocolate tarte. Then they switched. Brooke liked both desserts a lot. The carrot cake was moist and spiced just enough, though she would have done something differently with the chocolate tarte—maybe a little espresso would have perked up the chocolate flavor.

"These are incredible, but neither of them are as good as yours," Hunter declared once he'd had a taste of both.

Brooke laughed, her cheeks flushing. "I'm flattered."

Hunter grinned. "But seriously, they are. How did you get so good at baking? Did you go to culinary school?"

"Just a lot of practice at home. I almost went to culinary school, and sometimes I kick myself for not going for it and applying, but it's turned out better this way, I think." She shrugged and took another bite of carrot cake. "I learn better on my own."

"That's amazing," Hunter said. "So you learned from the ground up?"

"Yeah, pretty much literally. I started when I was really little." She took a sip of her decaf coffee, the warmth of the drink and the memory spreading through her chest. "My grandma was an amazing baker, and whenever we would stay with her for a weekend or over the holidays, she'd teach me something new."

Hunter nodded, urging her to go on and studying her face with curiosity.

"I was too small to even reach the countertop at first, and obviously I couldn't do anything with the oven or stove. So I stood on a stool and dumped things into the bowl, then helped her mix things up. And I licked the spoon, of course."

"That's the best part."

"It totally is." Brooke chuckled.

The memory of her grandma's little kitchen, with its ancient oven that heated unevenly and its pink laminate countertops, always stuck with her. Brooke had a picture of the two of them making cookies around Christmas when she was about five, which was in a little frame in her own kitchen.

"As I got older and learned some things on my own, I baked for things at school or for my family," she continued. "Once I graduated and went to college, I started to de-stress by doing it. Kneading dough will crank my stress down fast. People liked my food, but they were college students who were up for anything, so I didn't pursue it seriously."

"So what made you take it more seriously?" Hunter took a small bite of the chocolate tarte, leaving a perfectly sized bite for Brooke. He nodded for her to take it, and she did.

"I think it just came from time. I had all the basics down, and I liked to experiment with new flavors. Having a bakery was always a dream, but kind of like a kid wishes they could be an astronaut— it didn't feel attainable." She took a small forkful of the carrot cake, leaving the final bite for Hunter. "Then I watched Angela and Lydia open the Beachside Inn, and I figured that I could actually do it. I could make my dream come true, just like they had."

"We met at just the right time, then," Hunter said.

"Yeah, I think we did."

Brooke smiled, taking in Hunter's handsome face. She had never been on a date with a guy who listened to her as much as he did. His expressive eyes and the warmth that glowed in them when she talked about her future made her heart flip in her chest.

This was the best date she had ever been on, hands down.

After they finished dessert, Hunter paid and walked her outside.

"It's pretty cold, but do you want to walk a little

bit?" Hunter asked, pulling a wool hat out of his coat pocket.

"I'd love to."

He took her hand in his, and they walked toward the boardwalk, which was five minutes away. It brought Brooke back to their time at the movie premiere. The weather had been perfect for a walk there, much warmer than it was here, but she didn't even mind the cold that much. Hunter's warmth and their conversation made it easy for her to block any chill out of her mind.

They kept talking as they walked, never seeming to run out of topics of conversation or things to share with each other. Eventually, they turned around and headed back toward the restaurant to get Hunter's car. He drove her back to her apartment, then got out and walked her up to her door.

"This was really nice," Brooke said softly, fiddling with her keys as she looked up at him. "I had a great time."

"I did too." Hunter gave her that warm, boyish smile that she liked so much. "We should do this again sometime soon."

"We should. I'd like that a lot."

Taking a step closer, he cupped the side of her neck and leaned in, giving her a sweet, soft kiss. It was the perfect ending for a perfect night. As he pulled away, Brooke noticed just how quickly her heart was racing. It had been a long time since she'd felt that way after a kiss—and as she thought about it more, she realized no man had ever made her feel so special.

"Good night, Brooke," Hunter murmured, giving her another light peck.

"Good night."

He smiled at her one more time before turning and heading back to his car.

Brooke couldn't stop smiling either as she went inside and peeled off her layers, with Scratch winding his way between her legs in greeting. Everything with Hunter felt so real, so amazing. It felt so easy and right.

Between their growing relationship and the bakery, her life was transforming right in front of her eyes. Both of those things were new, and both felt life-changing.

CHAPTER EIGHTEEN

By early December, winter had really and truly arrived in Marigold. The temperature was well below freezing, and Angela hadn't quite adjusted yet. Getting out of bed that morning had been difficult, and even as the day wore on, she had to resist the urge to crawl back under the covers.

She slipped on her warmest socks and puttered around the kitchen, heating some leftover soup for a light lunch. Jake was with his grandparents, who were taking him to see a movie, so Angela had time to herself while Kathy and Lydia were manning the inn.

Her phone buzzed on the countertop, and she frowned a little in concern when she saw it was Scott. Her ex-husband had been in touch with her fairly frequently because of Jake, and they had regularly scheduled calls so Jake could see his father. Their next call was supposed to be tomorrow.

"Hey, Scott. What's up?" she asked, stirring her soup on the stove. "Is everything okay?"

"Everything's good. Great, even," Scott said with a chuckle. "I know our call with Jake is supposed to be tomorrow, but I wanted to give you some news ahead of time. It's pretty big."

Angela's throat tightened for a moment. Scott sounded happy, but that didn't mean he had news that was good for her or Jake. What if he was moving across the country, or doing something else that would uproot Jake's life when he went to stay with his father?

"What is it?" she asked, swallowing.

"I'm getting married again!"

"Oh, wow, Scott." Angela blinked, and her shoulders sagged in relief.

She hadn't been expecting him to say that, and she definitely hadn't expected him to find someone so soon. She had fallen out of love with Scott after he'd cheated on her and they had split up, so this didn't hurt her feelings like it might once have, when the pain of their separation was still fresh. But she was surprised that he'd gotten this serious with someone else so quickly. Their divorce hadn't been finalized for very long.

Angela smiled to herself. She had agonized for weeks about moving too fast with Patrick, but now she realized they weren't rushing things at all in comparison to Scott and his new fiancée. Then again, Scott was the type of man who needed to be married. He loved the idea of someone loving him, which was part of what had led to his infidelity in the first place. As much as Angela had tried, she hadn't been able to give him enough attention to keep his eye from wandering—and she shouldn't have had to compete with other women for his attention in the first place.

It was so different with Patrick, so natural. She didn't have to worry about him flirting with other women behind her back, and she never doubted his feelings for her. She and Patrick were falling for each other at just the right speed, and it wasn't like they felt the need to get married right away. It hadn't even come up, although she knew that they were serious about each other. She was crazy about him, and he was crazy about her, so why press ahead in a hurry? They were going to be together no matter what.

"Yeah, crazy, right?" Scott said, drawing her

focus back to the conversation. "She's really great. Her name is Cheryl."

"How did you two meet?" Angela asked. A flicker of worry flashed in her mind—what if he had met this new woman when the two of them had still been married?

"We met at a Fourth of July party this past summer and hit it off right away. She works in PR, and she's from Philly originally. I doubt we would have met if I hadn't decided to go to the party at the last minute," Scott said. "I want Jake to meet her on a call at some point so the change isn't too drastic. I wouldn't want to bring her to the airport with me and spring her on him."

"That would be lovely. Congratulations, Scott." And she meant it, too. "I wanted to have Christmas on the island, but I was thinking I could bring him to Philadelphia for the second half of his winter break. Maybe they could meet then."

"That sounds like a good plan," Scott said. "I've got to run, actually. I'm meeting Cheryl for lunch. Take care, okay?"

"You too."

Angela hung up and turned off the burner her soup was on. Talking to Scott made her realize just how much happier she was with Patrick. She felt like she could really be herself with him in a way she never really had when she was with Scott. She didn't have to worry about whether she was doing enough, or whether he was being dishonest.

She sat down with her soup and ate it while watching a little TV, then called Brooke.

"Hey, Jake is with Mom and Dad for the afternoon. Do you want to go Christmas shopping?" Angela asked, putting her bowl in the sink. "I have everything down for Jake and Mom, but I need a second opinion on gifts for Patrick. I want to get the perfect thing since it's our first Christmas together."

"Oh, I'd love to, but I'm kind of swamped with stuff for the bakery right now," Brooke said. "I just got some admin stuff in the mail that I have to tackle."

"So things are coming along?"

"Yeah! It's just coming along with a mountain of paperwork. It's a bit nerve-wracking." Brooke laughed, but Angela could hear the anxious edge in her voice, plus some fatigue.

"Do you need help? All of those forms and licenses and whatnot can be really overwhelming."

"No, I'm good, I promise."

Angela bit her lip and resisted the urge to insist on helping. That would only stress Brooke out more and might make her feel like Angela found her less than competent, as if she were unable to finish the work on her own.

"Okay, I'll see you later, then."

"See ya."

Angela got dressed and headed to the inn, finding Lydia at the front desk. Lydia grinned and straightened up.

"Welcome to the Beachside Inn. Are you checking in with us today?" Lydia said jokingly.

"Yup, I'm checking in to see if you're up for a bit of Christmas shopping." Angela rested her forearms on the desk.

"I'd love to. I'm so behind on my shopping list," Lydia said. "I'll text Kathy to work the front desk for a while. We were going to switch off soon anyway."

"Sounds like a plan."

* * *

Lydia shivered, tucking her hands into her pockets. Downtown Marigold was always elaborately decorated for the holidays, and this year was no different. There were wreaths in almost every window and sparkling lights everywhere, making everything inviting and festive. She wrapped her scarf around her neck one more time as she and Angela walked, trying to decide which shop to go into first.

"How about this boutique?" Angela asked.

"You read my mind. This place seems perfect for Grant." Lydia opened the door, the rush of heat from inside melting the chill on her skin.

Angela seemed to read her mind a lot. They were with each other almost every day, but only got closer instead of tired of each other. They'd been close in high school, but their friendship now felt better than ever. Maybe it was their maturity or just the circumstances, but there wasn't anyone else Lydia would rather go Christmas shopping with.

As always, Lydia was grateful for the chance meeting that had brought them together after all those years, which gave them the fresh start they'd both needed. Where would she be if she were still living in Boston? Mourning Paul, her ex-husband, instead of living boldly and adventurously like he'd told her to? The thought of that felt so foreign to her, like it was literally a past life.

The boutique had clothes and accessories for men and women, and both Lydia and Angela gravitated toward the men's side.

"I have no idea what to get Patrick," Angela said,

picking up some warm-looking socks and turning them in her hands. "He likes to be comfortable since he's usually home writing all the time, but I don't want to get him anything boring."

"Hey, getting socks for Christmas as a grown-up is great," Lydia said with a shrug. "I love practical gifts."

"So do I." Angela snorted. "My mom got me a paper shredder for Christmas last year, and I think I got more excited than Jake did when he opened his new LEGO set."

Both women laughed and wandered around the store a little more. Lydia found a warm vest that was perfect for Grant, who sometimes felt constricted by a heavy jacket when he was out with his landscaping team, and helped Angela pick between a nice, but casual cardigan and a hat for Patrick.

Angela went with the cardigan since was incredibly soft, and she thought Patrick would get a kick out of looking a little more literary. It had elbow patches and everything.

They went to a store that featured local crafts next and shopped for everyone else, even as a light dusting of snow started to come down outside. Lydia found a cute bag for Holly and a necklace for her aunt Millie, while Angela rounded out her shopping with some home decor for Travis and her parents, plus another small gift for Jake.

"This would look great on you," Lydia said, picking up a blue sweater. Then, she checked the price tag and sighed.

"Pricey?"

"Oh yeah."

"Maybe we could skip getting gifts for each other? We've already gotten a lot of stuff, and even though the inn's doing well, we should dial back on the spending," Angela said.

"Sounds like a good plan," Lydia replied. "Plus, it feels like the universe already gave me a lot of gifts this year."

"Same here." Angela grinned.

And it had. Lydia was beyond grateful for everything that had happened over the past year. Starting over again, finding love after her heart-shattering loss, starting a new career, and reconnecting with old friends was worth more than anything money could buy.

They left the store and the sweater behind and headed down the street to grab a bite to eat. The snow was still falling lightly, and the chill in the air had become more biting while they'd been inside the last shop. They picked the first restaurant they came across, which cocooned them in its warmth when they stepped inside. The hostess put them in a little booth in the corner, which gave them a great view of Christmas lights gleaming amidst the blustery day outside. The low lights in the restaurant made it all seem magical, as if they were looking out into a snow globe.

"I think it would be a crime to not get something braised," Angela said as she looked at the menu. "What do you think?"

"I totally agree. This weather calls for something that sticks around a while."

Both of them decided on braised short ribs and mashed potatoes, along with some mulled red wine. Their waiter put some bread down on the table too, fresh from the oven, which felt amazing in Lydia's chilled hands and even better when she tasted it. It was the perfect start to a holiday season meal.

"To our first Christmas at the inn?" Lydia asked, holding up her mug of mulled wine.

"I'll drink to that."

The two tapped their mugs together and smiled, settling in for another great meal together.

CHAPTER NINETEEN

Brooke's papers were covered in flour, and somehow, her big bag of flour was underneath several papers. She was inside her bakery—it felt great to finally call it hers—and she was trying to tackle one of ten thousand things she had to do before the opening. Everything was moving fast. Being inside and working made it feel so real, but so scary.

She looked around. Her equipment was all set up, although using it well would be a whole other story. She had wrestled with the industrial sized mixers, overworked some dough, and then decided to start it over. That new batch of dough hadn't turned out correctly either. Instead of light, fluffy bread, it was dense and impossible to enjoy.

Frustrated, she'd moved on to making cinnamon

scones, which she made literally every day. If someone asked her to make some in her sleep, she knew she could. She crossed her fingers as she peeked inside the oven to see how they were coming along. They were still pale on top.

It was so different than making everything at home or at the inn. She had always wanted more space to move around, but now that she had it, it overwhelmed her. Nothing was in arm's reach, so she'd rearranged the big stainless steel tables a few times to make things easier. It had sort of worked, but now she banged her hip on the table every time she went from one side of the kitchen to the other.

She checked over her to-do list since the scones seemed to be doing well. Paperwork. More paperwork. More marketing ideas, more spreadsheets. More of everything.

The familiar but unwelcome scent of over-baked food filled the air in an instant.

"No, no, no. Ugh!" Brooke yanked open the oven and took out her scones.

They looked fine on top, but when she lifted one, it was black on the bottom. She dropped the scone and pressed the heels of her hands against her eye sockets, holding in tears. How could something go from under-baked to burnt in half a second? She baked in her apartment's oven all the time, and it was ancient. How could she burn something in a brand new, state-of-the-art oven that had all the proper buttons and settings?

This was the fourth batch of scones that she had ruined, and she had been there all day trying. The breads she had tried didn't work, and the cookies she had tried to make were barely passable. She had to figure this out, and soon.

"Hey, I saw the light on," Hunter said, popping his head into the kitchen.

"Oh, hi," Brooke said, sniffling. "I didn't hear you come in the front door. I guess I should have put that bell on there. I'm a mess, sorry."

Hunter didn't even take his coat off—he crossed the kitchen and pulled her into his arms. All of the flour on Brooke's pink apron probably transferred onto his nice coat, but he didn't seem to care.

"Hey, what's wrong?"

"I don't know if I can do this. I've burnt or messed up literally every test batch I've made so far. Plus my to-do list is literally one mile long and getting longer, like it's growing on its own now." Brooke took a deep breath, taking in the subtle, clean scent of his cologne. "I feel like I suck at running a business, and now I'm starting to suck at baking too.

How can I suck at baking when I literally own a bakery?"

Hunter kissed her forehead, then lifted her chin to kiss her on the lips.

"It's going to be okay. I'm pretty sure that most business owners feel like they're floundering at least once. If they aren't, they're probably too cocky," he said. "Didn't you say that Lydia and Angela had a rough time opening the inn? Look at them now— they're doing great."

"That's true." Brooke dabbed at her eyes even though they were drying already. "It's just scary because I feel extra pressure now, since we're dating and all. Your money financed all of this, and I don't want to let it fail."

"Hey, I made a solid business decision when I invested in this place." He squeezed her waist. "I think it's a great idea. I didn't just do it because I like you. And I know it'll do well because those semi-burnt scones still look delicious."

Brooke chuckled and rested her head on his shoulder again. Hunter rubbed her back.

"And the business is totally separate from us as a couple," he added, gently nudging her to lift her head again. Brooke looked into his gray eyes. "I care about you, and that won't change. My feelings for you aren't dependent on how well this business does. If it tanks, I'll support you. If it succeeds, which I know it will, I'll support you. I'm in this with you for the long haul, Brooke."

She smiled, feeling teary for good reasons this time. His words touched a spot in her heart that was aching and raw. She'd had no idea how much she needed to hear that until he'd said it.

"Thank you," she murmured, pulling him in for another hug, then a kiss. "That means the world to me."

CHAPTER TWENTY

Lydia watched the ferry pull into Marigold's harbor, a grin on her face. Holly was finally coming home for her winter break and Lydia couldn't wait to see her. Lydia leaned back against Grant, who was rubbing her arms over her coat to keep her warm as he stood behind her. It was a smidgen too cold to be waiting outside, but Lydia didn't care.

"Holly, over here!" she called when she saw the top of her daughter's favorite pink hat.

Holly's face lit up when she spotted her and Grant, and the mother and daughter rushed toward each other, colliding in a hug that was padded by their coats.

"Hi, Mom! I missed you," Holly said into Lydia's

shoulder before separating and turning toward Grant. "Nice to see you again too!"

Grant hugged Holly, smiling broadly as he greeted her. Seeing the two of them say hello to each other so warmly and with such ease broadened the smile on Lydia's face. Grant had become a fixture in her life, so she was glad that her new beau and her daughter had taken to each other so quickly. Not that she'd had any big doubts that they would—Holly was great, and so was Grant.

But in the grief support group she'd gone to after Paul's death, she'd heard some stories about times when it didn't work out well, and she knew that she had lucked out. Sometimes kids struggled when they saw their parents move on, throwing off the dynamic at home and forcing the parent to make difficult decisions. If Holly had felt like that toward Grant, it would have been much harder to let go and fall for Grant the way she had. She loved both of them dearly.

Grant picked up Holly's suitcase and led them to his car, making small talk with Holly as he did. Holly laughed, and so did Grant. Lydia adored his laugh— it was low and grumbly, and it was always genuine. Holly caught them up a little on her trip to Marigold from Syracuse on the drive back to Grant's for dinner.

Grant had made amazing chili from fresh peppers that he got from his parents on a visit out to Arizona, which was warm and ready for them by the time they got back.

"Wow, that smells amazing," Holly said, taking a deep inhale as she grinned.

"It tastes just as good. We'll get the table set up, if you want to freshen up," Lydia said, shooing Holly down to the half bath down the hall from Grant's kitchen.

Lydia had eaten dinner at Grant's numerous times, but this was a first for Holly. It was nice to see her daughter in a new but familiar environment, and once Holly returned from washing up, they sat down at the table with the chili and jalapeño cornbread. Her daughter took a bite of the chili and blinked in surprise.

"Wow, that's amazing," Holly said, taking another bite. "It's got a nice heat, but not too spicy. And needless to say, it's a billion times better than the chili from dining hall on campus."

Lydia laughed and poured herself a glass of wine. "How did the end of the semester go? And how were finals?"

"It was really hard, so I'm glad it's over. I had more exams instead of papers this time, so I spent a lot of time huddled up in the library with some hot chocolate and my notes." Holly shuddered at the memory. "But I think I did well on everything, especially my education classes."

"That's good to hear. I'm sure you did well." Lydia served herself another slice of cornbread. "Did you get the chance to have some fun in between all those exams?"

"A little bit. My friends and I had a movie night to take a break, but all of us were so stressed out that we didn't really get into it much." Holly sighed. "But now I'm planning on relaxing as hard as I can."

Grant and Lydia laughed.

"It's some well-deserved rest," Grant said.

"And I got to FaceTime Nicolas a lot, too, especially since we were both up late studying. It was a nice break," Holly added.

"Oh? How is he?" Lydia asked.

She had met Holly's boyfriend at the end of the summer, when they'd both come back from studying abroad. He was Spanish, but he had dual citizenship between Spain and the United States. He had started going to school in Boston in the fall, having transferred there from his previous school overseas.

From her frequent phone calls with her daughter, Lydia knew that Holly and Nicolas were still together and were getting pretty serious.

"He's really good." Holly's expression warmed up. "We talk all the time, but it's been hard being long distance. He's been thinking about transferring up to Syracuse so we can be together."

Lydia nodded, hoping her nerves didn't show. It was clear that they adored each other, but they were both so young. Making a big life decision, uprooting yourself and moving to be closer to someone, was a big deal.

"Mom, you look like you just got an ice cube dropped down the back of your sweater," Holly said with a quiet snort.

"It's just..." Lydia gathered her thoughts, letting out a breath. "It's a big decision that has implications for you both. You're both so young with a bunch of life ahead of you. You know how I worry."

Grant took Lydia's hand and gave it a little squeeze, glancing between her and her daughter.

"It's their decision, and they're both smart," Grant said. "I think it'll be great."

Holly beamed at Grant, her brown eyes shining with happiness, and he gave her a smile in return.

Lydia's shoulders relaxed a little. Grant was right, and she knew he cared about Holly a lot. He was truthful too, so she knew he meant what he said about believing it would all work out. Whenever he had concerns, he was great at expressing his feelings in a levelheaded way, which always made Lydia's anxiety go down a bit.

"You're right," she acknowledged, squeezing Grant's hand back. Then she glanced at Holly, who was the spitting image of her late father with her dark hair and dimples. "I think I'll worry about you even when you're my age."

"That's because you're my mom." Holly smiled, her eyes soft. "I'd be worried if you didn't worry. Do you want to FaceTime with Nic after dinner, just to say hi?"

"That would be lovely," Lydia said. She was glad Grant was there to calm her nerves and keep her over-protective motherly instincts from getting out of hand.

They chatted about the inn and everything going on in Marigold as they finished up their chili. Lydia insisted that Holly sit down while she and Grant cleaned up, so Holly dialed up Nicolas while they cleared the table.

"Hey, Nic!" Holly said, holding her phone up in

front of her and waving. "How are you? I miss you so much."

"Hey, you," Nic said, his Spanish accent faint but noticeable. Lydia could tell he was smiling even though she couldn't see him. "I miss you, too."

"Do you want to say hi to my mom and Grant?" Holly asked, standing up. "We're just cleaning up from dinner."

"Yeah, of course."

Holly turned the phone to fit herself, Grant, and Lydia into the frame. The last time Lydia had seen him, Nicolas's brown hair had been longish and floppy, hanging down over his forehead a bit. He had cut it at some point since then, which made him look a little more mature. He also seemed far less nervous than he had been when they'd first met him when Holly had brought him back to Marigold with her.

"Hi, Nicolas!" Lydia said, waving as much as she could while staying in the frame. "How are things? Where did you go for winter break?"

"Things are good! I'm with my dad. How are you two?" he asked, sounding genuinely interested.

"We're pretty good." Lydia looked to Grant, who nodded in confirmation. "It's been nice here, and we've been getting into the Christmas spirit. The inn is pretty full, but we have more help now."

As Grant filled Nicolas in about how he was doing, a knot loosened in Lydia's chest. Nicolas was a nice, caring young man. He and Holly fit together well, supporting each other even from a distance. Lydia couldn't imagine a young guy caring about his girlfriend's family unless they were serious. He and Holly seemed pretty darn serious.

But they were still so young. Lydia remembered being twenty and thinking she had it all together when she didn't. But Holly was so bright and kind, so she hoped everything would work out for her daughter.

Holly eventually headed into the living room to chat with Nicolas one-on-one as Lydia and Grant finished putting away leftovers and tidying up. Grant ran his hand up Lydia's back and gently squeezed her tight neck muscles. She glanced up at him, finding a little concern in his eyes.

"Still nervous?" he asked quietly, massaging a muscle in her shoulder until it loosened.

"A bit. It's getting really serious between them, like they're in it for the long haul." Lydia scrubbed a pot a little bit. "But he's a good person. You like him, don't you?"

"I do. I think they'll be just fine." Grant kissed

Lydia on the temple and took the sponge from her. "Let me get this for you, honey."

Lydia glanced over at Holly, who was laughing at something Nicolas had said, and smiled ruefully. Young love was exciting, but for the parent of someone experiencing it for the first time, it could be nerve-wracking as well.

* * *

"Yes! Victory!" Brooke sang to herself as she pulled out a batch of scones from the oven in her bakery.

She hadn't even checked the bottoms yet, but she knew that they were absolutely perfect. She quickly peeked under one, relieved to see that it was exactly the golden color she had wanted it to be.

Finally.

After wrestling with the ovens and mixers for several days, she was finally getting the hang of it and the business in general. She had moved on from her tried-and-true recipes like her cinnamon scones to more experimental ones like this rosewater, pistachio, and cardamom mini scone.

She put the fresh-baked scones on a cooling rack to rest for a little bit while she fiddled with some doughs she had resting, then finally tasted one. A groan of happiness escaped her throat before she could stop herself. It was perfect. The rosewater, the trickiest ingredient, wasn't overpowering, and neither was the cardamom. It was all in perfect balance. She grabbed another one and headed out to the front, where Hunter was installing a shelf behind the counter.

"Whatever that is, it smells delicious," he said with a grin.

"Oh, it is. A rosewater, pistachio, and cardamom mini-scone." She held up the baked treat. "Open."

Hunter did as she asked, and she put a bit of the small scone in his mouth. He chewed for a moment, then grabbed the rest of the scone, nodding and giving her an enthusiastic thumbs up. He popped the rest in his mouth moments after.

"This is your best one yet," he commented, sounding like he meant every word.

"I'm so glad they turned out well! I've finally gotten a handle on these new ovens, thank goodness." Brooke beamed.

"I didn't mean the best ones in this kitchen." Hunter pulled Brooke into his arms, and she buried her face in the warmth of his chest, listening to his voice rumble in his chest. "I think they're the best ones of all time."

"Wait, really?" she asked, her face still pressed against his soft flannel shirt.

"Oh yeah. I think the one I just ate is even better than the very first scones I tried when you, Angela, and Lydia came to my house to convince me to not build a hotel on the island." Hunter smoothed a piece of hair that had fallen out of Brooke's ponytail behind her ear. "Which was a stupid idea, in retrospect. I think the scones started to knock a little sense into me. I can't imagine the island with a big hotel now."

"I'll be sure to give you scones whenever you have an idea that might be a little off the wall again." Brooke laughed and squeezed him a little tighter.

"Good. I need a good talking to sometimes." He kissed her forehead and let her go. "I'm happy things are turning out this way. If I had gotten approval for the hotel, we might not be here now with this bakery. And your bakery is so much better."

Brooke's heart warmed as she grinned. Hunter's endless support meant the world to her. Even at that first meeting, which had ended with him saying that he was going to go ahead and try to get re-zoning approval, she'd been able to see that he wasn't a bad guy. Lydia and Angela hadn't been so convinced—they'd just seen him as a rich movie star who wanted to come in and ruin everything. But now they saw what Brooke saw: a man who loved the island and the people on it as much as people who had lived there for their whole lives.

Brooke gave Hunter one more peck on the cheek before heading back into the kitchen to make another batch of scones that would hopefully blow his mind even more than before.

CHAPTER TWENTY-ONE

Angela mentally thanked herself for decorating the inn's common areas in colors that could easily shift from holiday to holiday. The main hall, as they called it, was all woods and dark blues, which went beautifully with the twinkling lights Patrick had helped her put up around the big window and the wreaths that she had hung up everywhere.

She adjusted a poinsettia plant in the middle of the table where they had put all the food for the Christmas party and stepped back to study the room. It looked great. They had replaced the fall and Halloween decor with nutcrackers, holly, and other festive knickknacks along with the new lights and the wreaths. With the snow falling outside, it felt even cozier than ever.

"It looks great!" Brooke exclaimed, coming in with a platter filled with Christmas cookies. She was wearing a fluffy green sweater than made her eyes look a little greener than their usual blue.

"Thanks! Those cookies look amazing, too." Angela snagged one before Brooke could even put the platter on the table. "Oh man, everyone is going to love these."

Brooke smiled. "You've had these almost every year for Christmas! It's the same recipe I make all the time."

"That still doesn't mean they're any less good." Angela finished off the small cookie, then she, Lydia, and Brooke continued making the final preparations for the party.

Soon, people started to arrive. They had invited all of the inn's guests and any Marigold residents who wanted to come. After their opening event at the beginning of the summer, they knew that they could pull in quite a few people. And they were right again—before Angela knew it, the main hall was filled with people, as were the other common areas. Classic Christmas songs played as people laughed, catching up with each other or meeting for the first time.

Angela and Lydia mingled, making sure that

everyone had drinks and topping off people's mulled wine, hot apple cider, or hot cocoa. The food was going quickly, too, especially Brooke's holiday treats, so they were in and out of the kitchen frequently, restocking platters from time to time. Finally, they got a chance to refill their own drinks and observe the party from the corner.

"The turn-out is great. I think this is even more people than we had for our grand opening event," Angela said, sipping her hot cider.

"Yeah, it is! Hopefully people see what this space could look like for their own parties," Lydia added.

The party was a great way to take care of two things at once—celebrating the holidays and showing how the inn could be a great entertainment space. They had already heard a little interest from guests, so Angela hoped that more weddings and parties were going to be in the inn's future.

The party continued to pick up, and more guests showed. Jennifer Lowry slipped into the room, shyly looking around, and Angela waved to the pretty real estate agent.

"Hey, Jennifer!" Angela said. "So glad you could make it!"

"Hi!" Jennifer broke into a relieved smile and

gave Angela a hug when she got close. "Wow, there are so many people here. I thought I was going to be unfashionably early."

"Nope, we're already in full swing." Lydia hugged Jennifer, too. "Do you want something to drink? We have regular wine, warm mulled wine, eggnog, hot cider, hot cocoa—which we can add a little splash of peppermint schnapps too, if you'd like."

"A regular hot cocoa would be lovely, thank you."

Lydia slipped away to get Jennifer her cocoa just as Brooke appeared with a fresh batch of cookies. Brooke waved, put the platter down, and came to say hello to Jennifer as well. All three of the women had become fond of Jennifer since she'd helped them find the perfect locations for their businesses. Inviting her to their holiday party was the least they could do to show their appreciation.

Lydia returned with the cocoa a few moments later, handing it to Jennifer with a smile.

"Wow, this is amazing," the chestnut-haired woman murmured after she took her first sip. "What's in it?"

"It's an old recipe from my aunt Millie," Lydia said. "It's basically just a liquified chocolate bar."

Jennifer took another sip and sighed, her light

brown eyes gleaming with satisfaction. "Wow. This is much better than any chocolate bar I've accidentally melted in my life."

The four women laughed. Angela was about to tell the story of how they'd botched a batch of the cocoa earlier, but then she caught sight of Travis standing near the food and drink table. He must've just arrived. She smiled widely and waved him over.

"Hey, merry early Christmas," Travis said, leaning down and giving her a one-armed hug, careful not to spill his cider.

"Merry Christmas!" She returned his hug, then stepped back. "Travis, this is Jennifer Lowry, our real estate agent. She helped us get the inn and helped Brooke get the bakery."

Instead of shaking Jennifer's hand like Angela expected him to, Travis just looked at the pretty woman in surprise. Jennifer looked equally shocked, her eyes going wide.

"I know Jennifer—we've met before," Travis said.

"Yeah, we have." Jennifer smiled. "I didn't know that you were Angela and Brooke's brother, although I guess I should have connected the fact that your last name is Collins."

"Oh, how did you guys meet?" Brooke asked, looking between the two of them.

"Travis came to help after I reported a break-in at one of the houses I was going to show several months ago." Jennifer glanced at Travis again. "He gave me his card to report any other weird break-ins, which was great, because there was another one in another house that my colleague was working."

"And we bumped into each other at a restaurant a while ago. Well, my date did." Travis shot Jennifer a lopsided grin, then looked down at his cup of hot cider.

"Small world!" Lydia said.

"Yeah, definitely."

Jennifer and Travis kept glancing at each other, as if they were curious about what the other person was doing. Angela couldn't help but connect the dots, her mind racing as she shifted her gaze from one to the other—were they interested in each other?

She noticed a flush creep into Jennifer's cheeks as the pretty real estate agent looked at Travis again.

Yes, there was definitely something there.

* * *

Travis was genuinely surprised to see Jennifer again. He had heard Brooke and Angela raving about their real estate agent, but had never made the connection that they were raving about Jennifer. It made sense, though. His sisters had loved how put-together and competent she was, and Jennifer gave Travis that vibe, too.

"We're so glad you could come to our little holiday party," Angela told Jennifer, snapping Travis out of his distraction.

"Thanks. I am too. And I brought a plus-one too, I hope that's okay. I came with my brother." Jennifer looked around the room until she spotted a man standing on the other side of the large open space. "He's over there."

Travis followed her gaze and saw the guy he had seen greet her at the restaurant. His whole body relaxed in relief, although he hadn't even realized until that he was tense.

The man was her brother, not her boyfriend.

Now that Travis was looking at him more closely, he could see the slight resemblance between them, and a flicker of excitement flared in his chest. Maybe Jennifer was single after all.

Angela and Brooke were eyeing him with that conspiratorial look that he was used to them giving him often. He had probably done a bad job of hiding his relief that Jennifer was single, at least to them. His sisters knew him too well.

"Oh, I think I see Jake's teacher over there," Angela said, looking between Brooke and Lydia with next to no subtlety. "Let's go talk to her."

"Hm? Okay." Lydia seemed confused, but Brooke clearly knew exactly what Angela was doing.

"Yes. Let's go say hi," she chirped, shooting Travis a grin before taking Lydia's elbow and steering her away.

"Talk to you later!" Jennifer said with a smile as the three other women disappeared into the crowd.

If Travis hadn't been interested in Jennifer, he would have glared daggers at his sisters for leaving them alone together so blatantly. But he didn't even care, because in this instance, his sisters weren't wrong. He was glad to have a chance to talk to Jennifer one-on-one for a bit. He'd always thought she was beautiful, but tonight, she looked particularly lovely. Her teal sweater dress highlighted her light brown eyes, and her hair brown fell around her shoulders in long, pretty waves.

"It really is a small world, huh?" Jennifer said, cupping her mug with both hands. "I feel like I know at least eighty percent of the people in this room in one way or another."

"Same here." Travis looked around the room. Neighbors, old friends, and friends of the family were peppered in the crowd. "I bet you meet a lot of people as a realtor, right?"

"Oh yeah. It's very much a word-of-mouth business." Jennifer sipped her cocoa. "It's nice, though. I like meeting new people and helping them find a place to call home. Or work, too. My brother was actually the one who suggested I get into the business since I'm a people person."

"That's great," Travis said. "Are you two close?"

"Yeah, we are. We hang out all the time. He was the one who suggested the restaurant where we ran into each other, actually." Jennifer looked at him over the edge of her mug as she took another drink of her cocoa. "Are you and your sisters close?"

"Yes, definitely. We've gotten even closer since Angela moved back here from Philadelphia. We have family dinners all the time. Sometimes I help Angela out at the inn when I have the time, and I was Brooke's number one taste tester before she found her boyfriend Hunter." Travis laughed. "I shouldn't have taken my position for granted. I miss having stacks and stacks of pies in my freezer and cookies whenever I wanted."

"Oh, I know, Brooke's cookies are amazing," Jennifer said with a dreamy sigh. "She baked a bunch for the realty office as a thank you for helping her buy the bakery, and they disappeared in ten minutes. I can't bake at all unless it's those tubes of cookies that you cut up and pop into the oven, so something freshly baked was a nice surprise."

"Yeah, her cookies are addictive." Travis smiled, studying Jennifer's face for a moment. He thought he would've gotten used to how pretty she was now that they'd run into each other several times, but the more they spoke, the more attractive she became. Maybe it was because it wasn't just her looks that drew him to her so much. Her bright personality shone through her features, making her look luminous. "I don't even attempt to bake. I can grill stuff and cook a few things, but I'm by far the worst cook in the family."

"You're probably being hard on yourself," Jennifer said. "I'm sure your cooking is great."

"Thanks for the vote of confidence." Travis grinned. "But everyone in my family is a great cook, so even an okay cook would pale in comparison. Our family dinner spreads are something else."

"That sounds so lovely," she said, sounding genuine in a way that made Travis's heart flip in his chest. "I've been sampling all the restaurants that are popping up on the island so I haven't had a big home-cooked meal in ages."

"Are you a foodie?"

"Mm, I guess you could call me that." A slight shadow came over her expression. It was the first time Travis had seen her look down. "I used to go out a lot with my ex since he didn't cook, so I'm still in the habit of it, I guess. Plus, it's easier to just grab take-out on the way home after a long day of walking around in heels."

"Yeah, I get that." Travis nodded and tried to think of a topic to shift to. Even mentioning her ex made the brightness within her dim, and he didn't like it. "Well, not the walking around in heels part. That would be pretty silly of me."

Jennifer laughed, warming right back up again. "I bet. It's even a little rough for me, but I fell into the habit of wearing them a long time ago. I used to work with another realtor who was very tall, so whenever she and I went to show homes together, I'd put them on so I wouldn't feel like I was surrounded by giants."

Travis chuckled, then watched her take the last sip of her cocoa.

"Do you want me to get you another one?" he asked, pointing to her empty mug. "I think they just put out more cocoa and some eggnog too."

"Sure, let's go."

Travis made his way toward the drink station,

Jennifer close behind. Just a brief conversation made him realize just how much his online dating paled in comparison. None of the conversations he'd had on his dates had felt as pleasant and easy. Jennifer was everything he wanted—smart, hardworking, kind, and of course, beautiful. But he could also tell that her ex was still weighing heavily on her mind. Maybe she wasn't ready to start dating again if she'd recently gotten out of a relationship.

Still, he made a mental note to delete his dating apps when he got the chance. He already knew that Jennifer was worth waiting for.

CHAPTER TWENTY-TWO

Hunter was glad he and Brooke were both wearing gloves, because his hands were sweating from nerves. He squeezed her hand as they walked toward her family's house for Christmas dinner. It was a picture-perfect day—snow on the ground, cold but clear in the low evening light, with all the houses and yards lined with decorations—so they had decided to walk instead of drive.

"You okay? You're squeezing my hand like you're afraid I'll get blown away," Brooke said.

"Hm? Sorry." Hunter relaxed his hand. "I'm just nervous about dinner and meeting your whole family."

"That's really sweet." She smiled up at him in the way that always made Hunter feel better, despite his nerves. "It's going to be fun, I promise. Everyone in my family is super friendly, and you've already met some of them."

Hunter nodded, letting out a breath. It fogged in the air in front of him. "It's just new. I don't have much family of my own since my dad passed and my mom and I aren't close. I just want them to like me."

Brooke stopped walking, her eyes soft, and pecked him gently on the lips.

"I promise you they'll adore you." She gave him an extra kiss for good measure, and they kept walking toward the house.

They finally reached the house, which had wreaths in every window and lights on all the bushes. Hunter could practically feel the warmth emanating from it, and the door hadn't even opened yet. Brooke knocked, and Hunter held her hand to steady himself.

"Hey there!" Mitch, her father, said when he opened the door. He was wearing a goofy reindeer sweater that went a long way toward putting Hunter at ease. It made the older man look a lot less intimidating, anyway. He shook Hunter's hand. "Nice to finally meet you, young man. Come in, it's chilly out there."

Mitch stepped aside and let them in. The whole

house was toasty and smelled delicious. It was brimming with life and chaos. Christmas music was barely audible over the sound of laughter, dishes clanging together, and good-natured discussion coming from the kitchen. Mitch took their coats and hung them on the rack by the door.

"Oh, there you are!" Phoebe called, appearing from around the corner. She was wearing a sweater with an elf on it, done in the same style as Mitch's reindeer sweater. Brooke's mother looked just like her, including her bright smile. "I'm so glad you're here! It's nice to meet you, Hunter."

She pulled him in for a big hug, as if she'd known him for years instead of just moments.

"Nice to meet you too. You have a lovely home," Hunter said, looking around. "It's beautiful."

And it truly was. The inside was just as well decorated as the outside, with a big, white tree in the corner and lights strung up along the ceiling. He could tell that Angela had probably had a hand in decorating, using her skills as an interior designer. Everything was tasteful and cozy.

"Let me take these from you. Come in, come in— do you two want some wine?" Phoebe took the bag that held the desserts Brooke had made and gestured for them to follow her.

"Wine sounds nice," Brooke said.

They walked toward the source of the delicious smell, past the dining room table that was set for dinner. The kitchen was packed with both people and dishes, with Lydia and Angela peering into the oven at the turkey, Mitch looking between a bottle of red and a bottle of white, and Patrick and Holly helping Jake with a gadget of some sort over in the corner.

The moment they walked in, Hunter was showered in welcomes and hellos that shattered the last bit of anxiety he'd had about the evening. Brooke adored her family, and he adored Brooke. Everything was going to be okay. He didn't have to turn on the charisma like was used to doing. This was different—every last person here was genuine and kind. He could be the real Hunter, not the movie star.

"Ooh, the desserts have arrived!" Angela said, grinning at her mother as she pulled out the desserts from the bag and put them on the big kitchen island. She reached for them, but her mother shooed her away.

"Hey now, no dessert before dinner!" Phoebe said with a laugh.

"We need to heat up the pies anyway. How else

will we get that nice melted ice cream on top of them?" Brooke asked.

As if on cue, Hunter's stomach growled loudly. Everyone burst into laughter, Hunter included.

"I guess that means we should hurry with the food! We don't want our guests to be hungry. Things should be done soon. We're just finishing up." Phoebe poured him and Brooke each a glass of wine, then shooed them into one of the living rooms, where Grant and Travis were nibbling on rolls and talking about football.

"Hey, you two. Did Mom banish you to the hungry people room?" Travis asked, standing and shaking Hunter's hand in greeting. Grant did the same.

"I guess so." Brooke sat down on the couch and patted the seat next to her for Hunter to sit. He did, putting his arm on the back of the couch. "I'm so excited to eat real food. I think I've been living off of test baking for the past week."

"How is that a bad thing?" Travis asked with a grin. "I miss being your primary taste tester. Hunter's stolen my gig."

Hunter laughed. "I have more than enough scones and cakes and cookies to last at least a year. I'd be more than happy to share my title—and my waistline would probably thank me."

"Can I get in on that too?" Grant asked with a chuckle. "Lydia brings me extras from the inn's breakfast when she can."

"You can all get as many treats as you want when the bakery opens," Brooke said, beaming.

"What's on the menu? Will it be like everything at the inn?" Travis asked.

"Some stuff, yeah, but I'm going to be making a lot more desserts," Brooke said. "For every day, there'll be your basic cupcakes and brownies, but I'm also going to have some rotating specials. I'll definitely bring the testers of those around, since I'll want feedback on them. I made some rosewater, pistachio, and cardamom mini-scones that were a big hit with Hunter, so they're going to be one of the specials early on."

"Those were incredible. I had no idea that rosewater would actually taste that good in a scone," Hunter said with a laugh.

"I think Brooke could put almost anything in a scone and make it taste good." Travis chuckled, and so did everyone else.

They continued chatting about how everything was going, including the new kitchen setup at the bakery, the transport van for deliveries that Brooke had arranged for, and the ups and downs of running a new business. Before Hunter knew it, they were being called into the dining room for dinner.

The spread was even better than he had dreamed it would be. Every single inch of the middle of the big table was loaded down with platters of food—four kinds of casseroles, two kinds of potatoes, ham, turkey, rolls, and so much more. It was like the Christmas dinner he had seen in movies growing up, but he'd never experienced one like this for himself.

As a child, his family's Christmas dinners had always been pretty minimal and uneventful, like they were just going through the motions to check it off a box. This feast felt like it had been put together with love and affection. He was excited to dig in.

He and Brooke sat across from each other, sandwiched between Angela, Jake, Patrick, and Phoebe. Mitch sat at the head of the table and took a quick look at everyone's hungry faces. He laughed, said grace briefly, and let everyone dive in.

Hunter didn't know where to start, so he got a little of everything. Brooke had described her family's amazing cooking skills in the past, but she had undersold them. It was the best food he'd had all year, hands down. The turkey was perfectly juicy, and the roasted potatoes had a nice crunch before they melted in his mouth.

He glanced up as he ate and caught Brooke's gaze as she took a bite of a roll, a smile in her eyes. As he grinned back at her, he wondered how he had ever worried about fitting in. There was nowhere else he'd rather be.

Phoebe couldn't take another bite of her dinner, and neither could anyone else—well, until dessert was served. Brooke had outdone herself this year with all the pies and desserts she had made, and Phoebe couldn't wait to try them. Luckily, there were enough cooks in the family that no one got saddled with all of the work, so they were able to create a massive feast as a joint effort. Christmas dinner was always stressful to put together, but it always went off well in the end. This year was no exception.

She looked around the table and smiled. All of her kids were happy and healthy, which was all she wanted in life.

Brooke was laughing at a joke Patrick had made, her blue eyes sparkling. Her youngest daughter was coming into her own, and Phoebe was so proud she could burst. All of Brooke's stressful days and late-night texts worrying about some aspect of her business would pay off soon. She was already so much more alive and filled with purpose than she had seemed before. Plus, she had Hunter at her side as support. He was laughing along with her, gazing at her with adoring eyes.

At first Phoebe had been wary of Hunter, given his movie star status, but he was a wonderful influence on Brooke. He fit right in with the family with his kindness and humble charm. It was always scary for her to see her kids building their own lives, finding partners and careers. As much as she wanted to protect them, she knew that they had to go out there and fail sometimes in order to grow more than she ever dreamed.

Angela was the prime example of that. She and Patrick were shoulder to shoulder, holding hands under the table, listening to Lydia tell a story. Phoebe had never liked Scott all that much, but Angela had seemed happy at first. When her marriage had fallen apart, the whole family had helped Angela pick up the pieces. Now she was running a successful business and was with a man who truly respected her.

Once Phoebe finished off her wine, she hopped

up and started to make room on the table for all of Brooke's desserts. Everyone pitched in, even though they were all moving a bit slowly, sated and happy and moments away from sliding into their own food comas. Phoebe's least favorite part of family dinner was doing the dishes, so she started on them while everyone took a few minutes to digest their food.

"Need help?" Travis asked, appearing in the kitchen behind her. "I can dry them."

"That would be great, hun. Thank you." She stepped aside so Travis would have space to work.

They washed and dried without speaking, and the sounds of Brooke prepping the desserts and everyone else chatting about how excited they were for it filled the air around them. Phoebe peered around Travis's shoulder when she heard Angela yelp, but Patrick had just pulled her into his lap by surprise. She smiled.

"They're good together, aren't they?" she said to Travis.

"Yeah, they are. He's a great guy." Travis gently put a platter down on the counter after he dried it. "And so is Hunter. It's nice to have more people around this year."

"It is." She looked up at her son. It was still hard to believe he was so much taller than her. Sometimes it still felt like he'd been just a little boy not long ago. "What about you? Will you be bringing anyone to meet us soon from those dating apps?"

"No, I got rid of the apps. They were all pretty awkward. It felt like everyone was trying to be someone else, which seems kind of weird when you're trying to find a person to spend your life with." Travis's ears went pink. "But..."

"But?"

"There's this woman I'm interested in, but she's not really on the market," he said in a rush. "Not because she's in a relationship or anything, but she doesn't really want to date right now. So I'm waiting for her. Although I'm not sure how long it'll be."

"She must be special, then. What's she like?"

"She's great—she's down to earth and kind. I've only met her a few times, but it seems like we have a similar outlook on life." His ears went even more pink, which Phoebe could hardly believe. "And she's pretty."

Phoebe peeled off her rubber glove and patted Travis on the shoulder. "She sounds perfect for you, and it seems like she's worth the wait. Don't worry. Life works out the way it's supposed to, you know?"

"Yeah." Travis smiled, his ears still pink in embarrassment. "Thanks, mom."

"Any time." She pulled him down and gave him a kiss on the cheek.

"Dessert's ready! Coffee too!" Brooke called to everyone as she took the last of the desserts to the table.

Phoebe waited for everyone else to go first since there was more than enough to go around. There was a chocolate caramel pecan pie, a blackberry pie, and a clementine cream pie, plus brownies and sugar cookies decorated like reindeer.

Once the coast was clear, she got herself some chocolate pecan pie and sat next to Mitch. She took a bite of the pie and sighed, the perfect balance and saltiness and sweetness taking over her senses. It looked like everyone else was enjoying their choices too.

Mitch looked at her with warmth in his eyes, then at everyone else at the table. She reached over and laced her fingers with him, and he rubbed a thumb over her knuckles. They were truly lucky to have such a loving family, and Phoebe tucked the image of everyone just like this, happy and content, into her mind for safekeeping.

CHAPTER TWENTY-THREE

"We're landing, Mommy! We're landing!" Jake said, leaning over to look out of the plane's window.

"Yes, we are," she said, gripping Patrick's hand a little tighter. Takeoffs and landings were her least favorite parts of flying. "We're almost there."

They were on their way to Philadelphia to drop Jake off with Scott for the week before he started back at school in Marigold again. Jake had enjoyed a great Christmas, so Angela hoped that he would have a good time with his dad and his new fiancée.

She squeezed Patrick's hand again before loosening her grip so she wouldn't crush his bones. She was glad he had offered to use some airline miles he had earned to come with her for support. Jake hadn't been apart from her for more than one night in his entire life, and she wasn't sure how it was going to go. Scott loved his son, of course, but she was anxious to meet Jake's future stepmother, Cheryl, in person. Angela hoped she was as nice as she'd seemed over the phone.

Once they got off the plane, they took a cab to Scott's new place, which was in a trendier part of town than their old house. They knocked on the door, and moments later, Scott appeared.

"Daddy!" Jake crowed, throwing his arms around Scott.

"Hey, buddy!" Scott hugged Jake, then stood back up and hugged Angela. He shook Patrick's hand last. "Hey, Angela. And nice to see you again, Patrick."

"Nice to see you, too."

"Come in. Cheryl's in the kitchen." Scott held the door open. "Honey, they're here!"

Scott's new home wasn't decorated as well as their family house had been—to Angela's admitted satisfaction—but it looked very "Scott." It looked the way his apartment had looked when he and Angela had first met: like a bachelor pad, with big leather seats and very few decor items.

"Hello, hello!" Cheryl called, appearing from around the corner. "So nice to meet you in person!"

Angela and Jake had met Cheryl over video chat a few times, but seeing her in person was different. She was slightly younger than Angela, with dyed red hair cut in a trendy way. Even though they were just relaxing at home, she was dressed up in designer jeans and an intricate blouse, her makeup completely done. Her engagement ring was massive and flashy, too.

Cheryl greeted Jake, who seemed happy to see her, to Angela's relief. Then she said hello to Patrick, who she hadn't met yet.

"Excuse me for seeming so frazzled," Cheryl said, smoothing her blouse. "I'm sure I look like a mess. I was putting something in the slow cooker for dinner."

"You aren't a mess at all," Angela said. "Your blouse is lovely."

"Thank you!" The red-haired woman beamed.

Angela smiled and resisted the urge to shake her head in bemusement. How could Cheryl think she looked like a mess because two hairs were out of place? Maybe Scott was drawn to women like that.

Angela helped Jake put his bag into his room, then they headed back into the foyer where everyone was waiting. Her heart sank a bit as they neared it. She was dreading waking up without

Jake, going about her day without being able to see him or tuck him in at night, but she knew that her little boy deserved to be with his father for a week. Scott was a great dad, even if he hadn't been a great husband. Angela was glad he was still in Jake's life.

"Okay, buddy," she said, crouching down to Jake's height. "Patrick and I are going to go back to Marigold. We'll see you soon, all right?"

"All right." Jake hugged her, and Angela held on for an extra few seconds. She heard him sniffle in her ear, and she blinked to clear the tears from her own eyes.

Jake hugged Patrick next, and Angela's tears threatened to spill over for another reason. She loved how the two of them had bonded—Jake cared for Patrick, and Patrick cared just as much for the little boy.

Not wanting to drag the moment out too much, Angela and Patrick said their goodbyes to Cheryl and Scott quickly, then headed out to the street to meet the car that would take them back to the airport. Their journey over had been filled with laughing and chatter, but the flight back was the opposite. Angela looked out the window as they flew, fully aware of the dark cloud that seemed to surround her. Patrick stole glances at her from time to time, putting his arm around her shoulders.

"Do you want to come over for dinner?" Patrick asked once they stepped off the plane in Marigold's small airport.

"Sure, that would be lovely." Angela wasn't very hungry, which usually happened when she was down, but she didn't want to be alone.

Patrick took her hand and held it all the way back to his house. He still had a few Christmas lights up around the door, but he had gotten rid of his tree. He sat her down at his kitchen table, which had some candles set out on it that she had never seen before, and kissed her on the forehead.

"Do you want any help?" she asked, starting to stand.

"Nope, not at all. Let me handle this." He gently pressed on her shoulder so that she would sit down again. "Besides, I'm making that risotto you liked. With the mushrooms and chicken."

She perked up a little at that. Patrick had made her this risotto once or twice before, and it was so good that she had asked him for the recipe. She had tried to make it herself a few times, but it always came out better when he made it.

"Really?"

"Yeah. You don't have to lift a finger for this—just let me handle everything." He smiled at her over his shoulder, then grabbed a bottle of white wine. It was Ladera Sauvignon Blanc, her favorite. "I knew you would probably need a little pick-me-up after dropping off Jake."

Angela finally smiled for the first time since they had dropped off her son, accepting the wine from Patrick. He started cooking after he lit the candles and turned down the lights a little bit, choosing some soft music to set the romantic mood more. After watching him cook for a little while, stirring the risotto with one hand and seasoning it with the other with practiced ease, Angela couldn't help but go to him.

She took over stirring for him, and when he turned toward her, she leaned up so that she could kiss him on the lips. He looked down at her with a smile in his eyes, then kissed her forehead again.

Angela felt so lucky to have a man like Patrick in her life. It was as if he knew exactly what she needed, even before she knew it herself.

* * *

Brooke had never interviewed anyone before, but she could guess that showing up to the meeting partially covered in flour wasn't a good move, even if she *was* interviewing someone to work at a bakery. But she might not have a choice—she'd lost track of time, and now her latest interviewee was gently knocking on the door.

"Coming, sorry!" Brooke called, whipping off her pink apron and throwing it onto a plastic-covered seat.

She weaved her way through the loveseats and tables that had haphazardly been put into the seating area without banging her toe once. She hadn't had the chance to arrange them yet, though it was on her never-ending list. She was in her big final push to open the bakery, so all she had left were the last touches—the layout, the register system, the advertising, and the launch day.

It was all overwhelming, but Brooke had slowly gotten used to the breakneck pace of running her own business. She knew she could make it happen.

"Hi, come in!" she said, opening the door. "Sorry to keep you waiting. Things are a bit of a mess around here! You're Gretchen, right?"

"No problem! I'm a little early," the woman said. She was a little younger than Brooke, with dark hair that she had pulled into a ponytail underneath her blue knit hat. "And yes, I'm Gretchen. So nice to meet you."

"Nice to meet you too!" Brooke waved her toward the back. "Let's talk in here where there are actual chairs to sit in and it's not such a mess."

They headed to the little office that was situated at the back of the kitchen and chatted about the job, which involved dealing with customers and helping with the baking. Gretchen seemed great—she had worked in a bakery in high school and was taking college classes online, so the hours would be a good fit for her too.

"Let's do a test bake to see how we work together," Brooke said, handing Gretchen an apron. "We'll keep it simple with some cinnamon scones. They'll be on the menu every day."

Gretchen nodded, her cheeks a little flushed with anxiety as she put the apron over her head. The test bake exercise was something that Cora, who owned the butcher shop on the island, had suggested to Brooke as a way to see if her employees could actually work well with her. It was a great idea. Brooke had already weeded out a few candidates because they weren't the best team players.

She had gotten a lot of amazing advice after she'd

accepted that it was okay to ask for help. Once she had, she'd kicked herself for not doing it sooner. Everyone was more than willing to give her a hand or answer a question, especially the other women from the entrepreneur group that Lydia's aunt Millie had brought together. She knew she would have imploded without them.

The front door jingled again, letting Brooke know that Hunter had arrived. He'd been here working alongside her every single day since she was getting close to the opening. She heard him start arranging furniture out front, but he didn't pop into the kitchen to say hi like usual—probably because he knew she was doing some interviews and didn't want to interrupt.

Gretchen followed Brooke's directions exactly and asked the right questions, weighing out ingredients carefully and keeping a positive attitude even when the mixers gave her trouble. By the time they finished the scones, Brooke knew that Gretchen was the one.

"Thanks so much. I'll get back to you tomorrow about my decision," she said, since Cora had also suggested that she sleep on any hiring decisions she made.

"Great, looking forward to hearing from you!"

Gretchen put her hat back on and headed into the cold again, giving Hunter a starry-eyed glance before she left.

Even though the novelty of a celebrity living in their midst had mostly worn off, some people still gawked at Hunter when they recognized him. Every time, he smiled back.

Brooke flopped onto one of the seats that was still wrapped in plastic, sliding down until her body squeaked against it. Hunter ran a warm hand over the top of her head, smoothing some hair that had fallen out of her ponytail away from her face.

"How'd the interview go?" he asked.

"Really well! I think she's the person I'm going to hire, but I'm going to sleep on it for a night." She looked up at him. "I can't believe I'll be someone's boss."

He grinned, his gray eyes twinkling. "I believe it."

"That's because you're the best." She sat up so she could give him a kiss. "Thank you, Hunter. I couldn't have done this without you. I feel like I'm running myself ragged as it is. If you weren't here, I'd probably be collapsed in a heap of flour, clutching my to-do list in a death grip and muttering nonsense to myself."

Hunter laughed and helped her to her feet. "Don't worry about it. I'll do everything I can to make sure the opening day goes off without a hitch. And all the days after, of course. What's left for us to do?"

"A lot. Mostly advertising stuff and preparing for the opening day, plus setting everything up in here." Brooke stretched. "I was also thinking about decorating for opening day with something special. I wanted to get some little paper lanterns with lights inside to decorate the windows, and maybe some cool balloons."

"That sounds like a great idea. It'll make everything more inviting."

"I hope so. But we should probably get the inside done first." Brooke laughed.

They worked late into the night, unpacking display trays, setting up the bathroom, and figuring out the best flow for foot traffic throughout the bakery. The next few days were the same, as was most of January. Every day, Brooke got up early to bake for the Beachside Inn at her bakery's much fancier kitchen, then delivered the goods in the cute van that she had purchased, just to get more practice driving a larger vehicle. Plus, it was free advertising since it was painted with the bakery's logo, which Kathy from the inn had designed.

It seemed like every day was a flurry of phone calls, checking emails, setting up the space, cleaning, and more. Brooke's feet ached, and she was certain she'd filled out more paperwork in the past few weeks than she'd ever done in her entire life up to that point. By the time she got home, long after dark had settled in, she usually ate dinner and passed out, only to do it all again the next day.

"It's been a long, long day, buddy," Brooke said to Scratch one evening when she got home from another day of preparation.

Scratch meowed back as if he understood her, and she grinned. All the time she spent talking to him had made the cat chatty. She gave him his dinner, then threw some pasta that Angela had brought over into the microwave for her own meal.

She flopped onto the couch and ate it while watching some mindless reality TV to wind down a little. Once she was done, Scratch hopped up on the couch and crawled into her lap. She rubbed his belly, then his ears, and stretched her legs. They weren't as sore as they had been when she'd first started working on the bakery, but they still ached a little from standing and running around all the time.

This was the hardest she had ever worked, but despite all the stress, it felt good. In fact, she had never been happier. Working on something that she cared about and loved, something she had built herself, hardly felt like work at all.

CHAPTER TWENTY-FOUR

Brooke's eyes popped open at five o'clock in the morning, ten minutes before her alarm was supposed to go off. It was a dark and cold February morning, but she didn't care. Today was the opening day of her bakery, and nothing could have kept her in bed for another second.

She took a shower and got dressed, putting on a little makeup and slicking her hair into a bun that wouldn't fall apart halfway through the day. Last of all, she slid her white button-down shirt on, which would coordinate well with the pink apron that was waiting for her at the bakery, and her favorite stretchy jeans. She studied herself in the mirror, smiling at her reflection. This was it.

"Wish me luck, Scratch!" she said, picking him

up and giving him a kiss on his furry little head. He meowed back and promptly hopped onto the windowsill to continue sleeping.

When she stepped outside into the dim morning, her street had the quiet peace that only new snow could bring. It fell gently, illuminated by the street lamps and the slowly rising sun, sparkling like glitter. She made her way to the bakery, buzzing with anticipation.

She'd thought she would be the first one to arrive, but as she approached, she saw Hunter standing outside in his down jacket, his cheeks reddened from the cold.

"Wait, stop right there," he said to her when she was halfway down the block.

"Why?" Brooke stopped, letting him walk toward her instead.

"Just trust me." Hunter gave her a quick kiss when he reached her and stepped behind her, covering her eyes with her hands. "Come on."

They walked forward slowly, taking care not to slip on the snow, until they came to a stop. Hunter turned her a little until she faced the building, then took his hands away from her eyes. Brooke teared up right away. She'd known she was going to cry today no matter what, since she was finally going to see her bakery, all ready to go just as she had dreamed about. But this was even better than she'd imagined.

Hunter had added a string of little purple lantern lights along the windows, along with some festive balloons.

Her heart swelled in her chest, filling her up with so much joy that she forgot to breathe for a moment. He had remembered. And he'd brought the rest of her vision to life, right down to the tiniest details.

"It's so perfect," Brooke murmured, turning to look at Hunter. "I can't believe you remembered the lights. I had such a hard time trying to find them, and I'd completely given up!"

"Well, I can be persistent when it's for a good cause. And I knew how much you wanted them." He chuckled and squeezed her shoulders before he stepped up to open the front door for her. "It was surprisingly hard to find lavender lantern lights, even online."

Brooke stepped inside and noticed even more little touches that Hunter had put together. There were fresh plants on some of the shelves, plus some bows along the glass between the customer and the baked goods. It was perfect.

"Thank you," she said throwing her arms around

him and squeezing him tightly. "This is the best thing I'd ever seen. I'm even more excited to open this place now than I was when I woke up, and I didn't think that was possible."

"I hardly did anything." Hunter kissed her temple and kept hugging her. "I just wanted to make everything exactly as you dreamed it would be, since your dreams are pretty amazing."

Brooke sniffed, holding back her tears, then laughed at herself. "Okay, I'm going to start crying and ruin my mascara if you don't stop being so sweet. Let's get started on setting up."

Hunter started setting up the signs for the pastry of the day, and Brooke headed to the back to start baking. Gretchen, the assistant she'd hired, arrived a few minutes later, excited to start. Brooke handed Gretchen her apron, then put on her own, which had her name embroidered on it.

Finally, it was time for Brooke's favorite part of the day—the baking.

She had planned out her menu of daily items, plus one opening day special, a chocolate cupcake filled with cherries and topped with dark chocolate buttercream, a riff on the cake she had made for Grant's birthday. It had been a hit at the party, so she'd decided to recreate it for the bakery.

She and Gretchen worked together seamlessly, baking the everyday muffins, scones, and pastries and taking them out to the display case for Hunter to arrange. Brooke lost herself in it, only checking the time when Gretchen brought it up. At eight o'clock on the dot, she rushed to the front door and unlocked it so that people could come in.

The bell rang not long after Brooke got back into the kitchen, and she grinned.

Her very first customer.

She swept some flour off her apron and headed out to stand behind the counter, smiling. Her first customer was a woman in her forties who appeared to be on her way to work. She was eyeing everything with an excited gleam in her eye.

"Good morning! Welcome to Brooke's Bakery!" Brooke said, smiling cheerfully. "What can I get you?"

The woman chose a muffin and congratulated Brooke on her grand opening before heading out into the snow-covered streets.

Brooke asked that question again and again as customers steadily trickled into the bakery. It was a little chaotic at first as she juggled the front and the back, re-upping on certain goods, talking to customers, and making hot drinks. Hunter helped too, taking over the register when Brooke or Gretchen were doing something else.

There was a brief lull before lunch, but then a line started to form with people who wanted something a little sweet and warm to take the edge off the cold February day. All of the networking she had done with the women in her entrepreneur group paid off—many of the customers had heard about the bakery through the other businesses.

"Cora!" Brooke called happily when she saw the butcher shop owner enter the bakery. "You made it!"

"I wouldn't have missed it for anything." Cora grinned. "It looks like things are going well."

"They are. It's chaotic, though." Brooke put her hand on Gretchen's shoulder as she made a customer some coffee. "But Gretchen here is amazing."

Gretchen thanked Brooke as her face flushed a bit. She waved at Cora before going to deliver the coffee to someone at one of the big cozy chairs.

"She's the one I hired after we did the baking test you suggested," Brooke said. "Thank you for the tip."

"No problem at all. I'm glad to see she's working out!" Cora glanced at everything behind the glass. "Did you guys make all of these together? What would you suggest? I'm in the mood for something with chocolate."

"We did! I strongly suggest the chocolate peanut butter cookies," Brooke said. "They've been selling well."

"I'll take three, then. I'll bring one to my husband. And eat two myself." She grinned widely, humor dancing in her eyes.

Brooke bagged up the cookies and rang Cora up. She thanked her one more time as she left, then again in her own head when she saw Gretchen laughing with a customer. She was so lucky to have found someone as good as Gretchen right away.

Phoebe and Mitch came by in the afternoon, looking around the place with obvious pride. Brooke had shooed her family away from the bakery in the last week before the opening so that they could be surprised by how it looked all put together. She was glad she had, because the expressions on her parents' faces were priceless.

"Brooke, it looks so beautiful!" Phoebe said when they got to the front of the line. "Congratulations, sweetheart."

"We're so proud of you," Mitch added. "And so excited to finally get another taste of those blondies. We haven't had them in a while."

Brooke laughed and went to pack some up for them. "I knew you'd want some. They're a part of our daily menu, so you can swing by and get one whenever you want."

"Looks like I'll have a lot of competition." Mitch took the bag and broke off a piece of his blondie. "It's so busy!"

"It is! Wait here a sec, I'll be right back." Brooke held a finger up to her parents to tell them to hold on for a moment, then went to handle the next customer in line.

Brooke chatted with her parents while Hunter took over the register, then again when the rest of her friends and family came by—Patrick, Angela, and Jake came after Jake got out of school, and Lydia and Grant came a little after them. Even Travis stopped by with one of his coworkers, getting a whole box of assorted goods to take back to the police station.

Brooke gave them all treats on the house to thank them for everything they'd done for her. It was just a small gesture, but she had no idea how to put her gratitude into words.

By the end of the day, it felt like Brooke had seen all of her friends, half of her high school class, and all of the business owners on the block. Her cheeks ached from smiling so much, and her feet ached because she hadn't sat down for more than three minutes at a time. But she didn't care. It was exhilarating and everything she had ever dreamed of.

The day slowly started to wind down, with the last of the customers who'd been sitting in the big pink cozy chairs saying that they'd be back again soon before heading home. Finally, only Brooke and Hunter were left. The snow had been falling steadily all day, creating a beautiful blanket over the downtown area. The street lamps illuminated the snow, just as they had that morning.

"And... we're done." Brooke let out a breath, turning the sign from open to closed and locking the door. "Day one is over."

Hunter pulled her into his arms and kissed her. He smelled like sugar mixed with his warm, spicy cologne when Brooke wrapped her arms around his waist for a hug.

"Congrats. You did amazing." He ran his hand up and down her back.

"Congrats to you too as an investor and all-around helper," she said. "You seriously saved us when things got busy."

"It was the least I could do."

"That's not true. You've already given so much!" Brooke released him, running her hands over his shoulders.

"I have one more thing to give you, actually." Hunter dug into his back pocket and pulled out a key with a piece of pink ribbon tied to it. Her jaw dropped, her eyes widening as he held it in front of her, resting in his palm. "My house has been pretty lonely without you. I'd like to change that if you're up for it. What do you say? Would you like to move in with me?"

Brooke took the key, beaming harder than she thought she could after a long day of smiling.

"Yes, I'd love to!" She gave him another hug and a kiss, her energy soaring again.

Hunter smiled too, his shoulders relaxing. She had hardly noticed it before, but he had clearly been a little nervous about asking her.

She grinned to herself. He had nothing to be nervous about. There was no way she would have said anything but yes.

They cleaned up, prepared for the next day, and then stepped outside and closed up the shop. Once it was locked, Hunter threaded his fingers between Brooke's and gave her a warm, loving look. She held his gaze for a moment, hardly able to comprehend that her day had ended on such a high note. She couldn't believe that her dreams had finally come true, with the added bonus of a man like Hunter by her side, supporting her all the way.

"Do you want to come to my place now?" he asked. "I know we won't be able to get you all the way moved in tonight, especially not after such a long day, but you could just pack what you need for the next day or two."

She nodded, happiness bubbling up inside her chest. "That sounds great."

"Perfect. Let's pick up Scratch and whatever you need from your place so we can go home," he said.

Brooke grinned, tugging him toward her apartment and their future. "I can't wait."

ABOUT THE AUTHOR

Fiona writes sweet, feel-good contemporary women's fiction and family sagas with a bit of romance.

She hopes her characters will start to feel like old friends as you follow them on their journeys of love, family, friendship, and new beginnings. Her heartwarming storylines and charming small-town beach settings are a particular favorite of readers.

When she's not writing, she loves eating good meals with friends, trying out new recipes, and finding the perfect glass of wine to pair them with. She lives on the East Coast with her husband and their two trouble-making dogs.

Follow her on her website, Facebook, or Bookbub.

Sign up to receive her newsletter, where you'll get free books, exclusive bonus content, and info on her new releases and sales!

ALSO BY FIONA BAKER

The Marigold Island Series

The Beachside Inn

Beachside Beginnings

Beachside Promises

Beachside Secrets

Beachside Memories

Beachside Weddings

Made in United States
North Haven, CT
07 October 2023

42483058R00168